As You Wish

JACKSON PEARCE

HARPER TEEN
An Imprint of HarperCollinsPublishers

HarperTeen is an imprint of HarperCollins Publishers.

As You Wish

Library of Congress Cataloging-in-Publication Data
Pearce, Jackson.
 As you wish / Jackson Pearce. — 1st ed.
  p.   cm.
 Summary: When a genie arrives to grant sixteen-year-old Viola's wish to feel she
belongs, as she did before her best friend/boyfriend announced that he is gay, her delay in
making wishes gives her and the mysterious Jinn time to fall in love.
 ISBN 978-0-06-166152-5
 [1. Self-esteem—Fiction.   2. Popularity—Fiction.   3. Genies—Fiction.   4. Wishes—
Fiction. 5. High   schools—Fiction. 6.   Schools—Fiction. 7.   Artists—Fiction.
8. Homosexuality—Fiction.]   I. Title.
 PZ7.P31482As   2009   2008044033
 [Fic]—dc22   CIP
                                                              AC

Typography by Jennifer Rozbruch
        09   10   11   12   13   LP/RRDB   10   9   8   7   6   5   4   3   2   1
                                    ❖

First Edition

For Papa

ONE

Viola Cohen

ALL I'VE LEARNED in today's Shakespeare class is: Sometimes you have to fall in love with the wrong person just so you can find the right person. A more useful lesson would've been: Sometimes the right person doesn't love you back. Or sometimes the right person is gay. Or sometimes you just aren't the right person.

Thanks for nothing, Shakespeare.

I pretend to read along—the key is to glance up at the teacher occasionally so you appear interested—but really, I'm watching a guy to my right. He slouches back in his chair, slack-jawed, wearing a black coat covered in safety pins. The tips of his hair are magenta, and he has a row of piercings in each ear. He's one of the Punk Guys, though he sometimes drifts into the Wannabe Skater crowd.

I squeeze my eyes a little so his face blurs—it's easier to imagine how I'd paint him if I let his features run together. My hands twitch, longing to hold a paintbrush instead of a pencil. A fan brush, probably, for the magenta spikes. I'd add a few shades of gray underneath his eyes to try to capture that sleepy, sullen look that all the Punk Guys seem to have.

Everyone in this classroom belongs to one clique or another—a few Pretty Girls, a few Druggies, a Smart Kid or two, a large handful of Emo Girls wearing plastic bracelets. I've studied them all semester, hoping to understand their looks, movements, voices—and then trying to paint it all later. Like if I can just get it down on canvas, I'll have the key to the social mystery of what makes them belong to something bigger than themselves. If I can figure out what it is that makes them belong, I can figure out why it is that I don't—why I've become an Invisible Girl. The kind of girl who has a handful of friends and a lot of acquaintances, but who doesn't really *belong* to anything. I guess being invisible is better than faking your way into belonging, but it doesn't feel any less lonely.

"So, basically, the moral of this play is, Wait until you see the person naked before you fall in love, just in case they have the wrong . . . equipment?" a voice says from across the room. The formerly drowsy class—including me—turns to pay close attention to the speaker.

"There's a little more to it, Aaron, but . . . yes," Miss Collins says, putting two fingers to her right temple. She's a young teacher, and she always looks scared when she has to talk about sex.

Aaron shrugs. "I guess I'll start asking girls to undress sooner."

We all laugh under our breath, and the teacher flushes. Aaron smiles—the kind of smile you usually see on Disney princes. He's the only one I know who could deliver that line and not get administrative detention for it. He's also the only one I know who somehow manages to belong to *everything*—his friends are the leaders of all the other cliques, the beautiful, high-school-famous people who seem to gravitate toward one another—the

Royal Family. I try to imagine the way Aaron's broad shoulders might look in watercolor. I wish I could figure out his secret—how to belong like he does. I wish I didn't feel invisible.

I sigh, wondering if I'll be doomed to walk home in the rain like I did yesterday, and turn to my left to glance out the window.

Dark brown eyes barrel into mine.

I suppress a gasp—there's supposed to be an open desk next to me. Where the hell did *he* come from?

The eyes belong to a golden-skinned boy who's sitting motionless like a cat preparing to attack a mouse. He's staring at me so intensely that I can actually feel his gaze boring into my skin. His eyes are deep like an animal's eyes—soft like a deer's, sort of, but also intense like a wolf's. Though I badly want to look away, I can't, as if there are ropes linking me to him. The stranger's skin sparkles even under the school's bland fluorescent lights as the sound of Miss Collins's voice drones on even more than usual. The world blurs at the edges of my vision.

Who is he? I blink furiously to try and make the rest of

the world come back into focus, but all I can see are his deep brown, watery irises. I'm drowning in them. This isn't right. I shiver and force my eyes away from his. It hurts, as if he'd had his fingers wrapped around my gaze.

I try to fixate on the whiteboard at the front of the classroom, but I can still feel his eyes on me. Chill bumps rise on my arms. I want to ignore him, yet another part of me desperately wants to look at him again. He had been looking at *me*, studying me, like I study everyone else. Why? I rub my lips together and carefully look back toward him, using a few strands of my hair as a shield between us.

But he's gone.

Not just from his desk—from the classroom. No one has touched the room's only door, but Strangerguy is nowhere to be seen.

I've finally lost my mind, haven't I?

I jump when the bell rings. Class is over. I crumple my sparse notes and shove them into my bag, then head for the door. The rest of the class is sprinting to the hallway; the faster you get into the hall, the longer you can be social before your next class. I linger a moment longer, thinking maybe Stranger-guy is just hiding behind a desk or something. But no—he's definitely gone. I exhale and duck through the doorway, hurrying through the baby-blue hallways to the commons. My best friend, Lawrence, is waiting for me, rerolling the sleeves of his designer shirt.

"Hey." Lawrence smiles as I arrive. He pauses and studies me carefully. "Something wrong?"

Lawrence can read me well—he's always been able to, even after we stopped dating seven months ago. Seven months and four days, to be exact. The day I became an Invisible Girl. Up until then, I thought I belonged to something amazing, something different—we were in love, after all. We were special. Without him, though . . . well, I don't really belong anywhere. Just another random Invisible Girl in a school hall, in the art room—even at home.

I shake my head at him. "I'm fine. Just tired." He gives me the "I don't believe you" look, and we head toward our next class. Every few seconds, someone waves emphatically at Lawrence—revealing his sexuality has elevated Lawrence's status from just a notch or two above mine to that of a full-fledged member of the school's Royal Family. Every girl wants a gay friend, I guess. Now he gets invited to parties, socials, TV nights—the sort of thing I end up hearing secondhand gossip about for weeks afterward. I ignore the waving and glance around the commons for someone new to study. Someone different. Someone I can analyze, pick apart in watercolors . . .

My stomach lurches.

It's him again—Strangerguy—leaning against the trophy case with an annoyed expression and an intense stare. With his golden-bright skin, he stands out like some sort of Persian prince in the crowd of mostly black and white faces. His glare is still unsettling, despite being strangely alluring. I grab Lawrence's shirt.

"Who is he?" I ask Lawrence through my teeth. Strangerguy runs a hand through his hair—his curls are almost ringlets, but not quite, and they hang around each finger like some kind of night-colored jewelry.

Lawrence follows my gaze, wrinkling his eyebrows. "What? Who?"

"Him! The guy over there by the trophy case." I look back in Strangerguy's direction, but he's vanished again. Not a trace of golden skin against the pale blue walls, no brown eyes to drown in.

My mind swirls. I think he—no, I *know* he was there. Lawrence gives me a worried look as we enter the science hall.

"You're sure you're okay?" Lawrence asks as we reach the door of my classroom.

"I guess so."

"Well, call me tonight, okay?"

"Of course," I answer—who else would I call? I hug Lawrence good-bye and turn into my biology classroom, which I'm relieved to see is totally void of Strangerguy.

But his absence doesn't last. By the end of the day, he's been around at every one of my class changes, in the back of two classrooms, and in the cafeteria at lunch. His stare gets ever more intense, and the allure has been entirely replaced with fear. And what's more, no one—*no one*—seems to see him other than me. People breeze by him in hallways. Teachers don't even glance his way during roll call.

It's like he's invisible. Actually, not "like"—I think he *is* invisible. Not the way I am; I mean really, *really* invisible.

Invisible. Like a movie special effect or a magic trick, only real—right in front of me, following me, *after* me. I try to convince myself I'm being irrational, but I can't think of any other explanation as to why the rest of the world seems oblivious to his existence—other than the notion that he's actually, genuinely *invisible*.

I've *got* to get out of here.

When the final bell rings, I dash through the halls and out the back door instead of to the art room. Seniors wheel out of the parking lot in bright cars with preordered graduation tassels on the rearview mirror, flicking ashes from their cigarettes and shouting to one another through open windows. I live only a half mile from the school, so I'm stuck walking home with the freshmen. I trudge past them all, head down, partially afraid that if I look up, I'll be accosted again by Strangerguy's stare.

My house is boring—two stories, blue shutters, piles of laundry throughout, and a fence out back that once housed a loyal golden retriever. And empty, since both my parents work now. I collapse onto the plaid living room couch. Lawrence is right. Too much time in the art room. I fold an afghan around my body and squeeze my eyes shut. But there's no way I can sleep—I keep picturing Strangerguy materializing beside me, all haunting eyes and silence.

I grab for the television remote and get sucked into some show—*100 Greatest Kid Stars*—which, though way more pop culture than I normally like, leaves me feeling pleasantly numb until my parents get home from work several hours later.

"Were you sleeping? Are you sick?" my mom says when she walks in the door and catches sight of the pillow lines on my face. I rise and meet her in the kitchen.

"Just stressed." Keep things short and simple, and they ask fewer questions. And, to be honest, I'd rather not try to explain Strangerguy to anyone, especially my parents.

My mom goes to the counter and begins opening boxes of Chinese takeout. "Stressed? Honey, you're sixteen. How much stress could you have? Pass me a fork—I hate chopsticks." She opens a can of Diet Coke and takes a long swig, then sighs. She looks at me and frowns as if remembering something.

"Wait, that's not what I meant. I meant to say: Would you like to communicate about what's stressing you out?"

"Um . . . no. Never mind," I say quickly, grabbing a box of egg rolls. In between work memos and romance novels, my mom has been skimming a book called *Reconnecting With Your Teenager*. I'm pretty sure that burning the book would help us "reconnect" more than reading it will, but self-help books are my mom's answer to everything, especially the fact that I don't want to talk to her about Lawrence. My mom shrugs and thumbs through the newspaper as I grab a few napkins, then retreat to my bedroom to eat.

When I was seven, I loved the color pink, and I begged my mom to paint my room this migraine-inducing color called Flamingo Dream, back before she returned to working full time. I wish she hadn't listened to me, because nine years later it's still Flamingo Dream. I yank my blinds shut; it sedates the pink a little. I fall onto my bed, which is covered in layers of old patchwork quilts and the stuffed animals I can't convince myself to put in the closet just yet.

I turn my head to look at the left side of the mattress. It's the side Lawrence slept on when I snuck him into my bedroom late at night. It was nice, falling asleep to the sound of his breathing. People assume Invisible Girls are the types who get straight As and are on the debate team or something. But we aren't. We want to be kissed and half undressed, before falling asleep next to someone we love, just like everyone else.

It's over. Let it go. My hand wanders to the empty side of the bed, playing with loose threads on the quilt.

"Look, can we stop this already?" A male voice blasts through the silence.

I scream so loud that my voice strains and cracks. My feet thrash as I fight with the quilts to find the floor, hair flying in front of my eyes and sticking to my face. I force my feet over the side of the bed, despite the fact that quilts are still snarled around my calves. Just as I find the floor, the pile of *Seventeen* magazines that I'm standing on slides; in a shredding of magazine paper, I yelp and collapse onto the carpet. Hard.

"Um, right," the voice says, irritated, but my heart is thudding against my chest so hard that I'm not embarrassed.

I frantically sort my legs out and peer over the bed, panting heavily.

He's leaning against my dresser in jeans and a beat-up black T-shirt, with both eyebrows raised. He has high cheekbones and a square jaw, and he's taller than I thought. The light glints off his animal-like eyes as his gaze locks on me in that expectant way I'm starting to recognize.

Strangerguy.

I can't yell for help because I've lost my voice in fear.

He folds his arms.

"Do you have a wish this time, or not?"

TWO

A Jinn

SHE SCREAMS.

Of course. Mortal females tend to do that. It just *had* to be a female again. There's nothing about this particular female that shouts "looking to summon a jinn," but then, there rarely is—my masters tend to be random. Wannabe pagan teenagers, young mothers, liver-spotted old men. They've all got wishes. This one in particular has straight, paintbrushlike hair. She's not fat, but I've granted "I wish I were thinner" wishes for females her size before.

There's nothing I can do until she calms down and stops shaking, so I lean back on her cluttered desk, knocking over a few bottles of nail polish. Seconds pass. Minutes. I shiver—I can feel myself aging here. Skin cells flake off my body, my hair grows slowly, millimeter by millimeter. My entire body is decomposing all around me, and there's nothing I can do to stop it. Another minute passes.

I sigh impatiently. I can't help it.

At least sighing gets a response from her. "Don't come any closer!" my master cries shakily. "I'll scream! My parents will come!"

So we're going to go this route?

"You've already screamed," I say, "and they can come, but since no one can see me but you, you'll look crazy. Just like you did at school when you tried to show me to your friend."

She grits her teeth. She's known about the invisibility since noon—I could tell when she figured it out—but hearing me confirm it scares her even more. She longs for me to be a stalker, because that fact would be easier for her to swallow than my truly being invisible. I can tell what she wants, feels, wishes for, just by watching the motion of her eyes, the way she moves her hands, the flick of her hair. Mortals give themselves away too easily. Everything they want is spelled out like words on a page, easy to read if only you know the language.

"Who are you?" she whispers, her voice brittle and frail.

"I don't have a name," I respond. "Call me whatever you want. But can we skip the formalities and hurry this up? I've been here more than seven hours already. Seven hours I'll never get back."

She folds her arms over her waist and backs up against the wall. "Hurry *what* up?"

I run a hand through my hair—if I hold onto it, I think it'll grow between my fingers like ivy. "With the wishes. What's the first one? I want to get back to Caliban, so if we can knock out all three wishes by—"

"What wishes?" The words explode off her tongue. She breathes heavily in the silence that follows.

Wow. She snapped.

All right. Try a different approach. Whatever it takes to get the wishes started.

"Let's start over." Light, think light, airy, bubbly, like those glittery female classmates she stares at. "I'm a jinn. I'm here to grant three wishes because you had a real, true wish today, and you lucked out. A jinn—that's me—was assigned to grant it. A wish in your Shakespeare class—of all places. You wished you didn't feel invisible, whatever the hell that means. So, it'd be super-great if you could make your wishes, say, immediately, because until you do I'm stuck here instead of in my own world. So, please, tell me what you wish for. You can do it. Just say 'I wish for great hair,' and we can get this thing rolling. *Master*," I tag on the end, rolling my eyes.

"Go . . . go away," she whispers, like she's warding off a bad dream.

"I'd love to. So wish three times, and after the third wish, you'll forget about me. You'll go about your happy little wish-laden life and I'll go back to Caliban. Come on. Just begin with 'I wish' . . . then you fill in the rest."

"What's Caliban?" she whispers.

Her question yanks at me, like being struck and dragged along the sand by a wave. I'm surprised that she's asking about something beyond wishes. But the tug is also a result of the bond that connects me to her. I can't avoid direct questions or orders from my master, and the more intensely a master wants answers, the harsher the wave feeling is. It rushes me, drowns my mind. I answer quickly to make the feeling go away.

"Caliban is my world, which I'd like to get back to, thanks, since I don't age there. Jinn age like humans while we're earthbound fulfilling wishes, so as of right now you've taken"—I glance at the clock—"seven hours and forty-six minutes from my life."

I can see her aging in front of me—every moment passes seamlessly into the next, but it leaves her a second older, a tiny bit different than she was before. She doesn't even realize it— mortals forget to notice that *time is passing*. She's changed so much since I first arrived—her hair is longer—her nails, too—not to mention the changes in her skin tone. I must have aged just as much. The thought makes me nauseous. So does the disbelieving, skeptical expression that crosses her face. Every moment she doubts me is another moment of my life gone. I bite my tongue.

"Look, I'll prove it." More desperate than I want to let on, I finally snap. She has the chance for all her dreams to come true, and she needs *proof*.

Ridiculous.

I point toward her with a sigh. One generic teenage girl wish, coming up. My master wraps her fingers around the lamp at her bedside, ready to fling it at me. My hands tense and feel warm as a swirling noise, like a tornado churning in her bedroom, echoes around her. Her fingers release the lamp, and her eyes close slowly as it clunks to the floor. She inhales deeply as the air around her begins to move, rearranging itself in spirals over her body. Her skin brightens, her hair becomes glossy and golden, her eyelashes lengthen, her stomach gets flatter. The way she looked before the Lawrence guy left her.

My master opens her eyes. She lifts her fingers and runs them across her lips cautiously. She looks at me, a wary expression on her face, and lets her hand slide down to touch her stomach. She sidesteps to look in a wicker-framed mirror, and I roll my eyes when a slow, sad smile crosses her lips. *Yes, this is what you want.* Well, sort of. Mortals always want something more—they wish for money, but what they're really after is to be carefree. Power when what they really want is control. Beauty when they want love. Sometimes they know it, sometimes they don't. I can't quite figure out what she's really after, but I've yet to have a teenage master who didn't want to look like the fake magazine people. It's kind of my default "See what you can have!" move.

Come on. Make the wish.

I grimace as she reaches toward her reflection. That's enough of that.

I nod toward my master, and a quick breeze sweeps around her. Her hair dulls to brown, her fingernails go back to being chewed and bitten, and her hips grow a little larger. She jumps back from the mirror, as if someone has punched her.

"What . . . what was that?" she whispers.

"You wanted proof that I'm real? There you go. It was just an illusion. But you can have that. Just wish for it," I prod.

She drops to her bed. Her eyes are wide, and chill bumps litter her shoulders.

Seven hours, fifty-three minutes.

My master is still quivering, but at seven hours and fifty-five minutes, her expression changes. Her eyes rise to meet mine, and before she says a word I already feel a rush of relief. She believes me. She doesn't *want* to believe me, but finally, she does. One step closer to a wish.

She speaks, her voice shaky. "So I should . . . I mean, if it's all real, then . . . I should wish for world peace or . . . or something."

I roll my eyes. *Some* jinn would trick her. They'd just smile and nod and let her go about wishing for world peace.

Why am I so nice?

"You can, sure, whatever. But it's a waste—wishes aren't permanent. If you wish for a million dollars, it'll be granted, but once you spend it, it's gone. If you wish for world peace, it'll be granted, but once someone fires a gun, it's gone. If you want your wishes to last, you have to wish for what will make you happy—not for *happiness*, because once it rains or your cat dies or something, it's gone. But for *something* that will *bring* you happiness. And you've got a half million wishes to choose from, so, please, pick one that will make you happy."

She sits on the bed and draws her knees to her chest. "Then I could . . . I could wish for . . ."

"Anything. Anything specific . . . ," I say anxiously. I glare at the clock on her dresser as another minute clicks by.

"But I don't *know* what could . . . make me happy. I don't know what could make me belong again—"

"Hair! Clothes! A new boyfriend, for all I care. Come on," I mutter. I should have just let her wish for world peace.

"Hair and clothes aren't going to stop me from being invisible," she says dejectedly. "If I could just . . . if I could be a part of something, something special. If I could *belong* . . . be something that's not just the hot gay guy's best friend or . . . something . . . something that would stop me from being invisible."

"Yes!" I cry with so much fake enthusiasm that it startles her into nearly leaping backward. "Wish for friends! Lots and lots of friends. I can do that. Just say the words, say 'I wish for friends,' and it'll happen. Reversing invisibility is easy—I can make them practically worship you."

"Well, no," she protests. "It isn't *them*, it's just . . . I mean, they're nice to me and all, but I don't really *belong* with them. They don't care if I'm hanging out with them or locked up in the art room. *I'm* the invisible one—"

"Yeah, okay," I cut her off. "Whatever you want. Let's do this." I clap my hands and rub them together, nodding.

She doesn't say anything.

Why isn't she saying anything?

I ball up my hands and inhale. "Any time now."

"Just like that?" she says feebly.

"Yes. Just like that." Another minute clicks by. She bites her lip nervously. "Okay, so then, you have . . . a problem with how incredibly, *painfully* easy this is?" I offer.

"Um . . . yes. I just . . . ," she replies, her voice barely a whisper.

I hold in a sigh. "And why is that?"

"It's just . . . just like that? I've been trying to belong again for seven months and four days but . . . just like that? I couldn't do it, I couldn't make it on my own, but now . . . just like that . . . I can?"

"You can thank me after you wish," I answer through gritted teeth.

"I . . . no. I can't just wish." Her voice changes, gets stronger. She narrows her eyes at me. "I'm not that pathetic. I don't have to wish for friends. I can't just wish and belong again."

"Yes, you—"

"No! I won't do it. Go away."

"I can't go away unless you wish!" I shout, my temper finally at its breaking point.

"And what happens if I *don't* wish?" she wheels back.

My breath freezes in my lungs. It was a direct question, so I have to reply. I swallow hard, hoping my voice won't quiver when I answer.

"Then I die." Saying it aloud makes it feel like I'm aging even faster, dying quicker than before. "If you don't wish, I'll age just like you, and I'll eventually die here, just like a mortal." I look to the ground, and when I bring myself to meet her eyes again I'm both relieved and ashamed to see a look of pity on her face. Pity. For a *jinn*. It isn't fair, mortals having such power over us. But still—please. Please wish.

"Okay," she says.

I'm unable to hold in a sigh of relief.

"I'll figure out what to wish," she continues. "I don't want . . . I don't want to make anyone die. But you won't die now, will you? I can think about it? Just for a little while. It's only, well, I don't know what to wish for. . . ."

I want to lie and tell her she must wish immediately, but once again, her question was direct, so I'm trapped. I nod reluctantly—no, I won't die right now. Her face relaxes.

"Fine. I'll be back when you have a wish," I mutter. It's not what I want to say. I want to explode, to yell, to tell her to wish now before another minute passes.

She nods, biting her lip.

I have to get out of here, before I say something that makes her hate me—if she hates me, she won't trust me, and if she doesn't trust me, she won't wish. The fabric-softener scent of her bedroom fades, and the liquidlike feeling of vanishing sweeps through me. The obnoxiously pink walls are replaced with cool night air; the hum of her fan, with the sound of crickets. I'm standing in the driveway now, and I look back at her house.

I run a hand through my hair. It's longer.

Damn.

There is no fear in Caliban. But one day here and suddenly I'm afraid for my life. I shake my head and fold my arms as the nighttime chill bites into me.

I hate this place.

Jinn don't sleep while earthbound, so while she enjoys a bed of giant quilts tonight, I have nothing better to do than wander the streets until she wakes up and thinks of a wish. I inhale deeply as I walk, even though the air tastes like the pollution that fills it. If I try hard—very hard—I can block the scent of Earth and think of Caliban at sunset. Caliban's sunsets are extraordinary: brilliant light beaming through the windows of an elegant city, illuminating the busy streets and tranquil gardens in a pale orange glow.

If she doesn't wish, I'll never get back.

No! I can't think like that. She'll wish. Besides, the ifrit won't allow that to happen. They can press her to wish, put her in a situation where she has to wish her way out—I bet I could help them figure out a press, even. I shouldn't be ashamed to ask for their help; it's their job, after all. Still, I've never had to ask before . . . something about the idea of putting in a request for a press is sort of embarrassing.

I stop and study my surroundings. I'm standing by an entrance sign that reads HOLLY PARK and is surrounded by wilting daisies. Ahead is a pool with a faded blue tarp sagging into the deep end, where the letters on the POOL RULES sign have been rearranged to spell curse words. Cigarette butts litter the sidewalk, and the pond far ahead is lined with weeping willows and graffiti-covered garbage cans. At the center of the park, however, is a single oak tree, standing tall and proud on a hill, branches fingering their way into the stars. It's just like the trees in Caliban—they grow tall but never old. I trudge toward it and collapse among its mossy roots.

There are no stars in Caliban. Or clouds. There's the sun and the moon, but never rain or snow or lightning or stars. In Caliban there isn't even much night—just sunsets that blur into sunrises and the day. There are parks like these, but none with sticky-letter curse words, and there are houses like my master's, but no horribly pink rooms. The city has skyscrapers, but no cars or smog. Thousands of jinn, but no disbelief or anger.

I have to get home. How do humans tolerate living on Earth, chained down by the mortality of their own bodies? The longing for Caliban floods me, filling my limbs and veins until I think I might explode from the pressure.

I have to get home.

THREE

Viola

THE ART ROOM is chilly, its stone floor littered with bits of paper and fragments of paraffin blocks. The walls are lined with stovetops and sinks—long ago it was the home economics room, before the school decided that teaching kids to cook is sexist. I guess it doesn't matter—it was replaced with the art program, and I can't cook anyway. It's six thirty on a Friday morning, so the school is almost completely silent, save the soft whir of the janitor waxing the floor a few halls down. A teacher shouts to a colleague in the hallway behind me—I jump at the sound of the voice. Worrying that a jinn might appear at any moment isn't good for the nerves. It wasn't good for my sleep schedule either—last night I slept for about an hour, tops.

Stop. Forget about him. Forget about wishes. Just focus on painting.

I set up several easels and pull out the paintings I'm working on for the Art Honors Expo that's coming up. The topic for the Expo this year is landscapes, and I can't convince myself that my mountain scenes don't need more trees or . . . something. I sit back, and my eyes wander to a set of easels on the opposite side of the room—Ollie Marquez's paintings.

I'm jealous, I admit it. I've been painting swamps, deserts, and mountains for the Expo. They're okay but nothing special. Ollie's paintings are way more creative—she's painted bedrooms in mountains, dining rooms underwater, and televisions on the edges of snowy lakes. I stand and walk toward them. Ollie used red, pink, neon orange. I used olive green and drab colors, thinking my pictures would look more like real nature. Whenever I try to be bold, to use colors like Ollie does, the paintings feel awkward and cheap, like knockoffs of Ollie Marquez originals.

It doesn't really matter that Ollie and I always win the same awards and are in the same art classes. Ollie is the *artist*. It's like

Ollie herself is a painting, an imported piece from a performance space in Manhattan, complete with hoop earrings and scarves in her hair.

And she paints with neon orange.

And she's dating Aaron Moor. They're king and queen of the Royal Family. Ollie's another beautiful person who belongs *everywhere*, who floats effortlessly among the crowds of people who adore her. I run my hand over the colors; they're carefree, sensual, reckless.

"Again? Really?"

I cringe at the voice.

"I don't have a wish," I gripe, turning to face the jinn.

He lifts himself onto the counter, his forearms flexing like bent amber, and then shrugs. "You have dozens, actually. You just refuse to make them."

"I'm not going to use a wish for something stupid," I mutter. I don't really know what's worse—the fact that I have these wishes for hair and clothes and belonging, or the fact that a stranger knows it. "Are you going to . . . I mean . . . are you going to be appearing and disappearing all day again?"

"I only come when you want me to or when you have a wish."

"So you . . . read my mind?" I say, nervous chill bumps rising on my arms.

The jinn rolls his eyes. "No. You're my master, so we're connected to each other until you make your wishes. You want me or you have a wish, I'm here—you don't even have to call for me out loud. I just *feel* it when you want me to show up. It's hard to explain. But I'm not a mind reader."

"Oh," I say, not entirely sure I understand.

"And if you don't want me here, just tell me to stay away. I can't disobey a direct order from you, master." There's a note of sarcasm—or is it remorse?—in his voice.

Master—the word makes me shiver. "Don't call me that," I say aloud. Hearing him say it is weird, like someone's calling me *sexy*.

The jinn raises an eyebrow. "What am I supposed to call you?"

"Viola?"

"We're not supposed to call our masters by name."

I stare at him nervously. I'm no one's master.

The jinn inhales deeply and rolls his eyes. "Fine, I'll call you *Viola*," he says. "I've been here nineteen hours now, *Viola*. You know, the name thing breaks the first protocol. I'm going to be in trouble when I get back."

"Thank you," I say sincerely. "And thank you for breaking . . . protocol?" I ask. He grimaces, like my question hurts him.

"There are three overarching protocols for earthbound jinn—respect one's master, be visible only to one's master, and return to Caliban as quickly as possible. So calling you by your first name is just one of the many ways to break the first one. There's an exhaustive list for each protocol. I'll get you a copy."

"Oh," I say, not sure if he's being sarcastic but certain that, protocol or not, I'm still not letting him call me *master*. It's creepy. "What happens if you break protocol?"

He sighs. "We're punished by the Ancient Jinn. Sometimes bound. You know that genie-in-a-lamp story? Just a jinn who broke protocol and was bound to a lamp in the middle of a desert. So I'd rather not break the rules, thanks."

"Oh. Then . . . um . . . it's just . . . the word *master* . . ." I struggle for words, trying to find middle ground so the jinn doesn't get stuck in a lamp and I don't have to be called *master*.

Finally, the jinn holds up his hands. "Whatever," he says, shaking his head in irritation. "I'll deal with the Ancients when I get back. *If* I get back."

I nod and step away from Ollie's paintings and toward my own, hoping the jinn will vanish again if I ignore him.

I run a finger across my own canvas affectionately. I love painting, even though I know I'm not exactly a brilliant artist—high-school good, maybe, but I'm no pro. But when I paint, it's like my emotions can fall through the brush, then be brightened up, toned down, manipulated, or hidden away. Everything about Lawrence, about being invisible, about wanting to belong . . . I can say it all on canvas in a way I could never say it aloud. When people ask about the paintings, I come up with some abstract meaning, but really, they're all just shouting about *me* in acrylic.

The jinn is watching me—I can feel his eyes on me. I inhale, trying to calm my nerves—I don't want him to see me like this: the sappy, emotional way I get whenever I start painting. It's like he's watching me undress. When I look back at him, he has a curious expression on his face.

"Sorry," he says quietly, so fast that it seems he forgot to be short with me. It surprises both of us, and I think if the jinn's skin were a little lighter, his cheeks would be red. The jinn looks away for a moment, then raises an eyebrow at my work. "You could wish to be a better painter, you know," he says firmly, folding his arms.

I shake my head at him. "It's not about being good. It's about being . . . passionate."

His mouth drops like he's about to say something, but he closes it again. I get the vague feeling I've impressed him. I try not to show my satisfaction.

I turn back to my canvas. "Look, when I have a wish, I'll—"

"Who are you talking to?" a voice interrupts. It isn't the jinn's.

I whirl around to see Lawrence standing at the art room

door, extension cords draped over one arm and a confused look on his face.

Awkward Moment Number One of the day.

"I . . ." I try not to look at the jinn, whose eyes are heavy on me.

Lawrence can't see him—*no one* else can see him, I remind myself. Don't make a fool of yourself in the art room, of all places.

"No one. What are you doing?" I ask, nodding to the cords.

"Lighting for the play, remember?"

"Oh, yeah—how's the show coming?"

"Horrible. The school board said that Rizzo can't have a pregnancy scare and Sandy isn't allowed to wear leather pants. And at the new, improved Rydell High School, there's no swearing, sex, or smoking." He steps from the doorway and drops the cords on a table.

"Sounds like family-friendly boredom." I grin. The jinn chuckles at the joke behind me, but of course Lawrence doesn't hear him.

"Pretty much. What can I say . . . the football team can practically be sponsored by Budweiser, but if the theater department shows a pregnant teen, all bets are off. I guarantee you they don't have these problems in New York. Thanks a lot, North Carolina." Lawrence nods at my paintings. "They look finished."

"Maybe. I've got another week to work on them, and they just aren't . . . I don't know . . . coming together the way I'd like. I think I'll come in this Sunday and spend the entire afternoon with them." I'm about to continue when Awkward Moment Number Two manifests, as bright laughter fills the hallway outside the art room. Lawrence and the jinn look to see the source, but I already know who it is.

Of all the mornings. They had to come in on a day when I've got a jinn following me around.

Ollie is traipsing down the hall toward the art room in a polka-dotted silk dress and long, plastic pearls. When she turns her back for a moment, a bright white tattoo of an artist's palette shines on her honey-colored skin. Ollie is trailed by Aaron Moor, who is sipping on cappuccino from the gas station. They pause in the hallway to kiss; it doesn't last long, but they press into each other and smile afterward in a way that makes me feel shaky. I was never one for PDA, even when I was with Lawrence, but right now I'd give anything to melt into someone like that.

"She looks almost like a female jinn," the jinn says, frowning when Ollie and Aaron kiss again. He jumps down from the counter and comes to stand behind me.

Of course she does—only Ollie Marquez could look like a supernatural creature. If girl jinn are as beautiful as the guys apparently are, Ollie is dead on.

Ollie smiles at me as they enter the art room—I force a smile in return despite the swirling nerves in my stomach. She goes to her paintings, while Aaron drops down in a chair. He kicks his feet up onto a table, and his eyes fall on me and Lawrence.

"Hey, Viola. Wish I'd known you would be in here—I would've picked you up some coffee," he says with a smile.

"You could wish he'd gotten you coffee!" the jinn adds. I try to both smile at Aaron and roll my eyes at the jinn—the resulting expression probably makes me look like I've lost my mind. Perfect.

"Dumott!" Aaron turns from me and calls out Lawrence's last name. They're friends—not like Lawrence and I are, but friendly enough because they're both high-school royalty. "What's with the extension cords?" Aaron asks.

"Lighting for the play. Aren't you doing sets for it?"

"Yeah, I'm trying to. Not a lot of time, lately."

"Too many parties?" Lawrence asks with a half grin.

Aaron laughs and Ollie nods. I try to look too busy sorting paints to answer, since my last "party" was my unicorn birthday bash when I turned eleven.

"He's charming, really. You should wish for him," the jinn says in a bored tone.

I've got a choice: ignore him or look crazy in front of Aaron. I've got to ignore the jinn.

"Your pieces look great, Viola," Ollie calls out from across the room. "I thought I'd finally come in and touch up mine."

"Thanks. I love yours, too," I reply while Ollie kneels to sort her neon-orange and pink paints. Jealousy rips through

38

me, both for the paint colors and for the way her dress flutters around her like water.

"You don't like her?" the jinn interrupts my thoughts.

"I like her fine. She's very nice," I mutter.

"Yeah, but that's why you don't like her." He grins, stepping closer to me. "You know, she *knows* who you are. The two guys *know* you. You're not as invisible as you think. So why don't you just ditch that particular wish and wish for a nice morning cappuccino instead?"

"Shut up," I mutter. He can't possibly be expected to understand that it's not about people knowing me—it's about not feeling like I *belong* with them. I shake my head at him in frustration as I turn away. "And you're wrong about Ollie. I like her," I whisper over my shoulder. I'm not sure if it's a lie or not—after all, Ollie is nice. And perfect. Everyone loves Ollie.

Breathe. Don't let him get to you. I exhale and stand up, only to see Lawrence eyeing me.

Awkward Moment Number Three. Lawrence raises an eyebrow, then starts toward me.

"You're in trouble," the jinn says, a hint of amusement in

39

his voice. It makes me want to punch him. Lawrence grabs my wrist as he passes me, dragging me along after him. Ollie and Aaron are too busy telling each other jokes between quick kisses to notice. The jinn ducks out of the way as Lawrence pulls me into the supply closet.

"You're hiding something from me, Viola Cohen," Lawrence says in a low voice. The scent of clay and old paint fills my throat as I inhale.

"You have no idea," the jinn answers as he leans on the doorframe. Lawrence, of course, doesn't hear him. I'd love to tell the jinn to get lost, but speaking to invisible people probably isn't going to make Lawrence any less suspicious.

"Whatever it is, Vi, you can tell me. It can't be any worse than anything I've told you. You're really going to keep secrets from your best friend?"

I have to hand it to Lawrence. He can really lay on a guilt trip. I shoot the jinn a bitter look through the dim light before speaking.

"If you had . . . let's just say, hypothetically, you had three wishes. What would you wish for?" I say.

"What?" Lawrence asks.

I collapse onto a stepladder with a loud sigh. Words begin to fall out of my mouth the way emotions usually fall from my paintbrush. I start with Shakespeare class, last night in my bedroom, this morning. Lawrence listens, expressionless, and the jinn shoots me doubtful looks.

When I finish, I feel both stupid and relieved. Surely Lawrence won't think I'm as insane as I feel. Though I guess I can't blame him if he does.

Lawrence kneels down beside me. "So . . . like a genie. You accidentally summoned a jinn?"

"Right. But now Jinn won't leave me alone till I wish."

"My name isn't Jinn, you know. That's like me calling you *Human*," the jinn says.

I don't answer. Instead, I look past him, staring at Ollie's tattoo through the open doorway to avoid looking at Jinn or Lawrence. Lawrence puts his fingers to my cheek and guides my gaze back to him. My throat tightens, like it does whenever Lawrence touches me like this. I pull away from his hand.

"So, why not just make some wishes so he leaves you alone?"

Lawrence asks. He still doesn't believe me—he's talking to me like an adult talks to an imaginative toddler.

"Wow. This guy, I like," Jinn says, moving away from the doorway and dropping down on my left, opposite Lawrence. "Listen to him, mas—er, Viola," he corrects himself. I sigh and look back to Lawrence.

"It's not that easy!" I snap.

"Sure it is. Just wish that Ollie was your best friend or something," Jinn says, peering at Ollie through the closet door.

"Shut up," I hiss.

"I didn't say anything!" Lawrence answers.

I feel my cheeks turn red.

"Oh. Talking to Jinn. I see," Lawrence says. I want to crumble—there's doubt in his voice, and it makes me feel as alone and scared as I did when we broke up.

"Lawrence! I'm serious!" I cry out. Lawrence takes my hand apologetically.

"No, no, I'm sorry. It's just . . . I mean, how can you be sixteen years old and have no idea what to wish for?" Lawrence asks, running a thumb over my hand.

"Exactly!" Jinn shouts. I ignore him and am about to speak when Lawrence jumps up. He takes several shaky steps backward, staring over my head, his mouth hanging open. I look at Lawrence for a moment before realizing that he's staring at Jinn, who is now slowly standing.

"He's . . . real . . ." Lawrence chokes on his words.

I exhale and nod. At least now Lawrence is crazy with me. Lawrence takes a half step forward and extends a hand to poke Jinn's shoulder. When his fingers make contact with Jinn's skin, Lawrence jumps. Jinn shrugs and gives yet another annoyed look—he has a lot of them, I've noticed.

"Wait, how come he can see you now?" I ask, rising from the stepladder.

"I *can* be seen by anyone, if I want to. I'm just not supposed to. It breaks the second protocol. But I sort of thought showing myself to him would get you to wish faster, so I could return to Caliban quicker, which is the *third* protocol . . . but somehow now I doubt he'll be any help." Jinn tilts his head toward

Lawrence, who pokes him in the shoulder again.

"A jinn. You just . . . wishes . . . and . . . ," Lawrence murmurs.

I nod. "I didn't mean to. Apparently one strong wish will do it."

"Well." Lawrence swallows hard and extends a hand to Jinn. "Good to meet you, then . . . Jinn." Jinn gives Lawrence a defeated look, then clasps his outstretched palm.

"Right. Think you can make her wish?" Jinn asks, nodding toward me.

"Good luck with that," Lawrence responds, grinning.

I roll my eyes at both of them and leave the supply closet. They follow me just as the bell rings, Lawrence still giving Jinn amazed looks. Aaron is helping Ollie shove paints into a drawer, but looks up when we reemerge.

"Lawrence, by the way—I'm having a party tomorrow night," Aaron calls across the room.

"What's the occasion?" Lawrence asks, his voice strained from trying to ignore Jinn.

"It's . . . uh . . . it's Saturday?" Aaron grins. Ollie laughs and

Lawrence nods. "You'll be there, right?"

"Yeah, sure thing," Lawrence answers. Aaron turns to me.

"Viola, you should come," he says.

I should come. I'm invited. My first instinct is to mutter no—I don't belong with the Royal Family. My lips part to make up a lame excuse about visiting my grandmother or something. But then Jinn steps into my line of sight, one eyebrow raised and an amused expression on his face.

I hate that expression. I want to show that expression that I don't need to wish in order to belong anywhere. Here I am, getting invited to a party—I can have friends on my own, without the hair or clothes or shoes, without a wish. I just have to say yes.

I just have to have the guts to go.

"Yeah," I say quietly. I repeat myself, louder. "Yeah. I'll go. Thanks for inviting me."

Take that, genie-boy.

FOUR
Jinn

I WATCH VIOLA opening packets of food that I'm very grateful don't exist in Caliban. How can an entire meal be microwaveable? No wonder these humans age. Consuming things like that probably takes five years off your life instantly.

Another day of my life is gone, without so much as a hint that Viola will wish anytime soon. I'm a *good* jinn. I grant wishes well—I don't play with the wording, don't trick my masters. I keep it simple. I try to give them what they really want. And this is my reward—sitting in my master's kitchen, because she's decided that not knowing where I am "creeps her out."

Mortals.

"Do you eat?"

I look over my shoulder at her. She's changed again—her skin is slightly different, and her fingernails are the tiniest bit longer. I scan the room to see who she's speaking to, but there's no one.

"Yes? No? Jinn?" she asks.

"Me?"

She nods. "Eat. You know, as in food? As in, would you like me to make you a Hot Pocket while I'm fixing one for myself?"

"I, er, no. I mean, I eat in Caliban. And I sleep there. I just . . . not here."

I've never heard of a master offering to cook for his or her jinn before. It's just not done. Does it break the first protocol, about respecting one's master? I'm not sure . . . I really should start carrying that *Pocket Guide of Jinn Protocol* around with me. How much trouble am I already in with the Ancients? They aren't exactly known for being lenient. I wonder if it's a problem that she's calling me Jinn. I have to admit, it's nicer to hear than "Hey, you!"

She shrugs and breezes past me to the living room, "food" and a canned drink in hand. I follow—normally, I'd wait for the order to do so, but since she rarely gives them, I've gotten used to assuming what she wants. She collapses onto the couch and grabs a pad of scribbled-on paper from the coffee table. I lower myself into an old armchair on the opposite side of the room, grimacing at the scent of aged leather. Everything in this place reminds me of time.

She stares at the paper blankly.

Being mortal must be terribly boring.

"It's my speech. For the Expo next week," she says, glancing up at me. "We have to talk about our paintings. How stupid is that? Isn't the point of paintings that they say what you don't want to say aloud?"

"I thought the point of paintings was being passionate," I reply, leaning back when Viola changes again. Her hair got a little longer, perhaps, or her eyes a little darker. It's difficult to pinpoint.

She laughs, so casually that it startles me. Masters don't . . . *laugh* at things I say. They make wishes. I grant them. Then I go home.

"Here," she says, and tosses me the television remote.

"Um, thanks." Masters definitely don't invite jinn to watch television with them.

My thoughts wander as I hit the POWER button, memories of Caliban flowing through my head. Mostly of me sitting in my apartment, watching the flower-lined streets and the green and silver city below—half metropolis, half garden, but all glittering and brilliant. My apartment was smaller, but it had a wide balcony that overlooked the sparkling city below and the mountains on the horizon—nothing like the cramped, musty apartments I've seen in this world. I close my eyes and remember walking in parks of flowering hyacinths and snapdragons, eating curried vegetables and jasmine rice, gazing at the lights of the skyline. . . .

Sigh. I have to stop lingering on thoughts of home. It's only making me feel worse. I open my eyes and look to the television. A familiar face appears on the screen.

"Hey! I know him! He's one of my former masters."

Viola looks up from her paper. "Who?"

"The guy in the long coat. He knew all his wishes right away. I was back to Caliban in twenty minutes." I don't remember his name—in fact, come to think of it, I've never known a master's name before now.

Viola's eyes widen and she blinks at the screen. "Keanu Reeves?" she asks in amazement.

I nod.

"What did he wish for?"

"Isn't it obvious?" I say, waving a hand at the screen. "Fame."

"That's why he's famous? Because of a wish?"

"Have you seen his movies? Surely you didn't think he made it on *his* acting skills?" I grant wishes; I don't work miracles.

Viola looks back at the screen, eyes screwed up in awe. "I guess that makes sense," she says faintly as my former master delivers a line poorly. "Wow."

"I tried to convince him to wish to be a good actor instead of wishing to be a famous actor but he said good actors don't always become famous," I add.

Viola changes again. "What other wishes have you granted?"

Her direct question pulls at me, but it's not overpowering; she's just asking, not demanding an answer. *A nice change from most masters,* I think, before I respond, "Just your standard things, mostly. Money, success, love. I brought a dog back from the dead once for this woman, that was interesting—strange wish, I thought, but it made her really happy. I shouldn't be telling you this either. First protocol, I think. But, hey, maybe revealing their wishes will give you some ideas."

"You brought a dog back?" Viola asks. "That's . . . that's a wonderful wish."

"I suppose." I play it off, but to be honest, it was one of my favorite wishes as well.

"So there's nothing you can't grant? No rules?" Viola says.

I shrug. "Sort of. Well, no, I guess there are a few. I can't grant wishes for more wishes. Oh—and I can't make you a mermaid."

"Um . . . what?" Viola asks, raising her eyebrows and smiling a little.

51

"A few years ago I had this master who was a dolphin trainer or whale trainer or something. Anyhow, she wanted me to make her a mermaid."

"And those Ancients you keep talking about have strict no-mermaid rules?"

"No. But I can't change what a person *is*. Just *how* they are, if that makes sense."

"Oh. Was she sad when you couldn't do it?"

"My master?" I ask in surprise. "I guess so. I think she might have cried. I don't really know ..." I trail off, somehow ashamed of the fact that I don't have an answer to Viola's question.

She smiles at me, and her eyes are full of a kind of sweet sadness as she lets her hair fall in front of her face. It traps me for just a second, and I almost miss the wish that passes through her gaze. I can't quite make the wish out—it's something deep, something she hasn't told me—something I get the feeling she hasn't told anybody. How can I not see it in her?

"What is it?" I ask. I'm usually so good at reading mortals ...

Viola presses her lips together and avoids my eyes. "I don't have wishes like that. I mean, I know what I want to wish for—to belong somewhere, to something, with someone. But I want to belong only so I can . . . feel complete again, instead of broken apart from losing Lawrence—"

"He's still your friend, you didn't lose—"

"Yes," she cuts me off. "I did. I didn't lose *him*, really, but . . . I lost something. Some part of me broke when I realized I wasn't loved anymore, that I couldn't love *him* like before. But I can't just make a wish to feel complete again— you said it won't last, that wishing to be happy never lasts. So the thing that would make me feel complete is belonging instead of feeling invisible, but I don't want to wish to belong. I can't be that pathetic, that I have to wish for something like that." Her voice gets smaller. "I just don't know."

I laugh. I don't mean to, but I can't help it—no wonder I can't read the wish in her. It isn't a real wish.

Viola's eyes flash angrily. "I'm glad you think it's funny."

I chuckle again. "Well, it's just that it's impossible to be a broken or whole person. You can only be a *person*. You can only exist, you can only belong to yourself, and you can only be responsible for your own happiness or belonging or what-ever. That broken-part-piece-whole thing is just a trick of the mortal mind. Three wishes won't make you feel any more whole than you already do. At least not for long."

I expect her to shoot back a reply and tell me off like she tends to. But instead, her eyes graze the ground, watery and rimmed in something between hurt and shame. She turns back to her paper.

I cringe.

She's just a mortal. I shouldn't feel guilty over a mortal. It's her own fault she has a fake wish. But several silent moments pass, and my stomach begins to feel knotted.

Fine.

"I wasn't laughing at you," I mutter. *There. Happy now?*

She doesn't look up.

"Don't get mad. I have to hand it to you, you're tough—most people would've made the wish to belong by now. I'm just saying that even if you wish for it, you won't feel any dif-ferent unless you can find the *thing* that will make you . . . belong."

"You don't understand," she says with an intensity I've never heard before. "You probably just sit around Caliban all day where everyone is perfect and whole and . . . what do you do all day there anyway? How could I expect you to understand?" She shakes her head at me.

Viola doesn't realize she's given me two direct questions. To be honest, I could avoid answering both; she doesn't really expect answers, so they don't pull at me. Still, I roll my eyes and answer even though I'd rather not—maybe it'll make me feel less guilty.

"Your parents are out for their anniversary?" I ask uncomfortably, turning to stare at the movie.

The question gets Viola's attention. She looks up and nods, while I try to fixate on Keanu as he bends spoons on the television.

This is so embarrassing. Maybe I should've stuck with the guilt.

"Did he get her flowers?" I look over at her. She nods again, and the wish for someone to bring her flowers darts to the front of her eyes. As usual, she doesn't say the wish aloud.

Mortal pride. I fight the urge to roll my eyes, and continue instead. "What kind?"

"Roses. They were on the counter when I got home right before . . . I called you."

"What color?" I ask.

"Light pink, I think."

I look down at my hands as I answer. "Light pink. That's . . . gentility, admiration, and grace. Unless he meant them as a pastel, because pastel roses are for friendship. And if they were more coral-colored than pink, it was for desire. That's what I 'do all day' in Caliban. I deliver bouquets for the florist." I wait to hear her make fun of me—most of the other jinn do.

Instead, several moments of silence pass. I finally raise my head to see Viola staring at me with a puzzled expression.

"You're a flower boy?" she asks. The corners of her mouth twitch in a poorly hidden smile.

"I'm a *bouquet deliverer*—forget it, I shouldn't have said anything!" I growl. This is what you get for having conversations with your master.

"No, don't be mad," she says, but there are hints of laughter in her throat—deep laughter, different from the bubbly way she laughs around people at school. Her face sparkles in amusement. "It's not like that. It's just not what I expected you to do. But why a bouquet deliverer? It pays well?"

I put my head in my hand. I should never have tried to explain. She wants an answer, badly, and though I try to ignore her, the questions pull at me until the wave feeling is too much to bear.

"No, it doesn't pay well. It doesn't pay at all, actually—we don't work for money, we work because we like our jobs. I like it because . . ." I grimace and sigh. "Jinn don't fall in love or attach to one another, like humans do. We're immortal in Caliban, so falling in love for an eternity is just . . . unrealistic. But for that one moment when they're getting flowers, it's like that doesn't matter. It's the only moment where they don't care that the jinn who sent the flowers will be replaced by another lover in a week. It's . . . different. It's this one instant when someone isn't just another random jinn, but is something special to someone else. So I like being the one who delivers the flowers so I see it, that's all."

I wait a beat before meeting her eyes, but when I do, her face is no longer twitching in amusement. Instead, her lips are curved in a gentle smile. "That's beautiful," she says. "Though it sounds sort of lonely."

I pause. "I've never really thought of that before. I wouldn't call it lonely. We just aren't . . . needy. Mortals need to attach because you have sadness and desires and a limited time to live. We don't have that there. . . ." I trail off, unsure if I'm making any sense.

Viola nods. "So do you send flowers to anyone?"

"No, actually," I say, surprising myself—I haven't thought of sending flowers in ages. "Female jinn are a little self-obsessed and . . . uh . . . grabby. I haven't dated in years."

"But you're so charming!" she replies. I raise an eyebrow, then catch the sarcastic glimmer in her grin.

It's hard not to laugh when her eyes are sparkling with amusement at her own joke. "Yeah, yeah. It's different there, though. We aren't chained to one another like everyone here is. You have yourself, your own identity. So long as you know who you are, you can be happy, so there's really no need to date—unless you're bored."

Viola chews on her pen cap through a wry grin. "Yeah. Or maybe you just can't get a date."

I sigh, but smile. "Okay, fine. You could wish for flowers, you know."

"Not gonna happen."

"How about flowers *and* chocolate?"

"Nope."

"Who doesn't like chocolate? A heart-shaped box of candy would make anyone feel whole," I say.

"Come on," she responds, "be reasonable. We aren't talking about choosing between left and right. Choosing three wishes is a huge deal."

"For you. Not for Keanu."

"Well, of course not. Everything is easy for Keanu. The guy can dodge bullets," Viola says.

A loud, grinding sound—the garage door opening—cuts her off. Her parents are noisy getting out of the car, like they've had a lot of wine at dinner. Viola looks at me as she rises from the couch.

"I'm going to my room. They're going to want to watch C-SPAN or something," she says.

I stand and shove my hands in my pockets. She doesn't want me in her bedroom again just yet, I can tell, but at least her fear of me has melted away.

"So I need to leave?" I say, even though I already see her answer. She looks apologetic, but nods. "All right," I say, and the room blurs as I begin to vanish. "Good night, Viola."

FIVE HOURS TILL the party.

Four.

Three. I should have spent the day painting—time always goes faster that way. I begin rooting through my closet, wondering what I'm supposed to wear tonight.

"You could wish for a new wardrobe." Jinn's voice comes from behind me. I don't jump this time—I guess I've gotten used to him appearing and disappearing. I sigh and turn away from my scant collection of outfits, meeting his eyes as I fall into my computer chair.

"Right, a new wardrobe. A worthy use of a wish. What

do girls wear to parties in Caliban, anyway?" I ask. "Do they dress up?"

"I guess. Or dress *down*, rather. They don't wear a lot to parties. . . ." I raise both eyebrows. Jinn shrugs and continues. "All jinn girls sort of look the same, though, so there's no real point."

"You're so romantic." I smirk and then laugh when Jinn fakes a gentlemanly bow before collapsing onto my bed.

"Yeah, well, to be honest, you sort of stop noticing the difference between one jinn and another after a while. We don't have names, and we all look pretty similar—it gets tricky to keep everyone straight, much less feel romantic about one in particular."

"That's so bizarre, to think of you not having a name. You're *Jinn*," I say. Who else would he be without that title? It somehow blows my mind.

Jinn laughs, then answers brightly, "I guess. Though that's just a name you gave me. When I get back to Caliban, I'll just be another jinn again—" He cuts himself off, and his eyebrows furrow in a puzzled expression that I don't totally understand.

I'm about to ask what he's thinking when he speaks again. "Anyway, female jinn go to parties half naked. It's not as appealing as you'd expect, but it's what the Ancients want." He begins picking at my quilt with a bored expression.

"Whoa, back up," I say, shaking my head. "The Ancients want jinn girls to be half naked?"

"Well . . . sort of. There aren't many jinn left—I think there are a few thousand of us. That's why they've got the protocol and everything; all the rules are an attempt to keep us from dying out."

"And naked jinn girls prevent genocide?"

"No, but it encourages . . . um . . . reproduction."

I cringe. "Sorry I asked. I thought you were immortal, though?"

"In Caliban. But all these little mortal world visits where we age add up, after a while."

"Oh," I say, swallowing hard to try to hide my guilt. Jinn shrugs and winds a loose thread around his fingers. I finally turn back to my computer screen, clicking through images of the new arrivals at the Gap. I look back to my closet with a sigh—I have nothing that looks like these clothes. I really need to go shopping more than once a year.

To add insult to injury, when Lawrence arrives to pick me up, he looks like he just stepped out of a fashion magazine. He carries the strong scent of coffee from a day spent working at a local coffeehouse, but he somehow makes it smell like expensive cologne instead of mochachinos.

"Wear the black," Lawrence advises once I've paraded my outfit options for him.

Jinn, who has been idly sorting through my stuffed animals, looks up at me. "I like the black, too," he says, then begins arranging the toys so all the cats are with other cats.

Lawrence looks at Jinn and shrugs. "Then it's unanimous. Wear the black. And come on, it's time to go."

What I wouldn't give for a paintbrush right now.

Arriving at the party is like showing up to a bizarre Hollywood premiere: I know all the stars, but only a handful know me. I watch them all, studying them, trying to figure out the best way to capture this giant blur of light and red and dance and beer. Red cups are scattered over the front yard, and all the doors and windows are open. Something inside crashes, followed by the twittering laughter of several girls. Music is playing so loudly that it makes my heart vibrate. There are so many cars parked in the yard and on the street that we have to pass the house and park almost a block away, where I can still hear the music pounding.

"Why am I here?" Jinn mutters as we walk through the darkness toward the brilliantly lit house.

"Moral support?" I answer with a smirk.

"Go, Team Viola!" Jinn says, doing a little cheer with his arms.

I laugh. "Fine, go then." The words fall from my mouth before I realize he'll take it as a direct order. I meet Jinn's eyes. "I mean . . . unless you want to stay."

Jinn raises his eyes at me. "Eh, I'll stay. Who knows, tonight might be the night you decide to make a wish."

"Speaking of wishes, Vi, you could wish I'd remembered to bring money for the beer," Lawrence says as he picks through his wallet, littering the ground in crumpled receipts.

"Whatever. I'm sure we can get in," he adds after meeting my eyes—I can feel my eyebrows wrinkling in concern.

Lawrence heads toward the house, nodding to the two barely dressed girls who flank the door holding buckets stuffed with dollar bills. The girls wave at Lawrence, all sparkly teeth and plastic jewelry, and I see him pointing to his empty wallet. But when he nods at me, their expressions fall.

"I mean, we can't let you *both* in for free . . . that's sort of the point of the Beer Buckets," one says. Does she think that I can't hear her? That I didn't see her face change when she saw me?

Jinn mutters and rolls his eyes. "Say you can pay."

I shake my head at him quickly, hoping the girls won't notice, but Jinn pushes me forward, lurching me toward them. I give the girls a look I know is pathetic and desperate. But instead of the looks of disgust I expect, one of the girls reaches toward me and swipes at thin air, then drops her hand into the bucket of money.

"Thanks! Go on in," she says in a cheerful voice. Lawrence looks surprised but smiles and steps inside the house.

I freeze.

"Illusion," Jinn explains. "They all saw you give her money. Blonde on a power trip, if you ask me. . . ."

"Thank you, Jinn," I whisper sincerely as we step through the doorway. I touch his hand briefly in appreciation; his eyes jump to mine in surprise.

"I didn't come all this way to walk back down the block," Jinn replies, yet his voice lacks the edge I was expecting. I glance back just in time to see a look of disgust and regret on his face as he scans the party he just got me into.

The inside of the house is filled with the malty sweet scent of cigarette smoke and spilled beer. It's loud, dark, and muggy; I feel sweat trickling down my back from the heat of the crowd. Everyone is standing in small circles, talking and leaning on one another: girls in fuchsia and turquoise with perfect straight teeth and boys with well-styled hair and coy grins. Aaron waves at us from across the room. He's motioning us to come over. I smile, and Lawrence puts a hand firmly on my shoulder.

"Do you want me to stay with you, Vi?" Lawrence asks. "Er—*us* to stay with you?" he modifies when he remembers Jinn. It's no secret to me that Lawrence is worried about me being here—he doesn't think it's my "thing." Maybe he's right, because part of me wants to wrap my arm around him until my nerves die down.

But no. I don't want to be Lawrence Dumott's Invisible Girl shadow anymore. I want to belong with these people on my own. And besides—this is Lawrence's party, too. I can't insist he babysit me all night.

"No," I say, hoping my voice sounds more confident than I feel.

Lawrence nods. "Well, if you need me, I'll be out back. Jinn? Coming with me? Or did you want to watch Aaron smash beer cans on his head?"

I roll my eyes at Lawrence, and Jinn gives me a questioning glance. "Go with Lawrence," I sigh. I'm about to correct the order when Jinn holds up his hands with an appreciative nod.

"I know. Not an order. It isn't as strong when you don't really mean the command." He glances at Aaron warily, then follows Lawrence, weaving through a couple of girls who are dancing with one another to give some guys nearby a cheap thrill.

"Viola!" Aaron waves again. He's surrounded by bleached blondes who give me dull, bored looks. I push through the girls (who, thankfully, make no attempts to dance with me). I catch sight of Ollie's golden skin on the opposite side of the room, where she sips a peach-colored wine cooler that matches her tank top.

"Sit down! I'll have someone get you a beer," Aaron says warmly. The faces of the girls around him darken. Are they *jealous* of me? No. That's impossible.

I inhale deeply and nod at Aaron. "That'd be great, thanks."

"Hey! Jason!" Aaron yells over the thick noise of gossip and music. A burly football-player type turns around. Aaron holds up two fingers, and the guy shoves his hand into the closest cooler, then tosses both cans over the coffee table. Aaron catches one after the other and hands a can to me.

I don't like beer. I've had it only once or twice before, and I sort of think it tastes like rubbing alcohol. But I'm not about to refuse one here—I pop the can open and try to pour it down my throat, to avoid tasting it all too much. Aaron turns away from me, distracted by a joke a willowy girl is sharing. I glance at the girl on my other side, but I can't figure out how to start a conversation with her. She probably doesn't even know who I am anyway.

Find something to say, Viola. Find something to do. I sink farther back into the couch. Maybe it can swallow me, so I don't look like a silent loser sitting here all awkward and shy. Maybe I should leave.

No.

I want to belong. I need to belong. I *can* belong. Without a wish. I exhale and force myself to sit up straight. I lean forward to glimpse Jinn and Lawrence sitting together on the patio. They're here—one is invisible, true, but still. If they can do this, I can do this. I tap Aaron's shoulder lightly, forcing a confident smile as he turns to face me.

SIX

Jinn

I FOLLOW LAWRENCE through a thick cloud of people and cigarette smoke, past a kitchen full of coolers and a few couples groping while they think no one is looking. Lawrence holds the door to the deck open for me. I glance back to Viola, who is just lowering herself onto the couch beside Aaron. She's fine. Besides, if she has a wish, she'll call me . . . no sense in me hanging around.

Why am I so concerned?

A girl calls out to Lawrence and rushes over. She starts talking fast—Lawrence looks like he wants to run from her. I look up at the scattered stars that peek out from behind a thick layer of clouds. Minutes pass—maybe longer. I've begun losing track of the exact count.

The unofficial goal for all jinn is to get three wishes granted in three days: "Three in Three." I've never fallen short before now—this is day three, and there's not a wish in sight. The deep sick feeling of aging isn't as strong as it was, but I can still feel moments ticking by, and I can still see Lawrence changing fluidly in front of me. I wonder what's happened in Caliban since I've been gone. Not much, I imagine—Caliban is sort of a smooth-running machine, really. Very few surprises—the Ancients make sure of that.

"Jinn?" Lawrence whispers sharply, and I suddenly realize he's been talking to me for the past minute or so. Thoughts of Caliban fade away and I lift myself onto the deck railing. *Jinn.* He considers it my name, just like Viola does.

"Sorry. I forgot you can see me," I answer.

"No problem. You've just been totally silent for a half hour."

"That long?" Wow. I really am losing track. "How long is this thing going to last?" I ask.

"A few hours. Just long enough for her to realize keg

parties aren't her thing, hopefully."

"You go to them," I respond. "They're your thing?"

"No, not really. I mean, I don't hate them. At first it was cool to get invited and to be there and everything. Now it's all just . . ." He shrugs. "Vi . . . this is no place for her. It's not that I don't want her to feel like she belongs again. I do, and I want to help. I just don't want her to do it like this. I've tried telling her she isn't invisible, that she can belong to whatever and whoever she wants, but after how I hurt her, I guess I have no right to stop her from doing whatever it is she thinks will make her happy."

Finally. From Lawrence emerges a wish. In the time I've been around him, he hasn't had a single wish—unusual for a mortal. But now the wish is clear in the way his eyes graze the floor: a wish to end his regret.

"What happened with you two?" I ask.

"The person who will be granting her wishes should know, I guess," Lawrence says with a forced smile. A few of the chattering girls are looking at Lawrence, their penciled-in eyebrows raised—he appears to be talking to himself.

"Rehearsing lines for a play," Lawrence tells them quickly. They look doubtful, but shrug it off.

Lawrence sighs and begins, "Viola and I were best friends growing up. When we were freshmen in high school, we decided to try dating. It was weird and wonderful all at once, because we weren't really nervous around each other, you know? It just seemed natural that we'd end up together, like the best friends always do in romance movies.

"I loved Viola, but I was starting to realize that it was in a different way than she loved me. I loved the security, having her there to talk to, having someone who understood me, someone I understood. As a friend. So one night Viola tells me she loves me, and we kiss, and I know that this time it's going to go much further than kissing."

"But you're—" I start.

"Gay. Yes. I am. And I shared that information with her right around the time she took off her shirt," Lawrence finishes, grimacing. He picks at the leaves of a nearby potted plant.

"Great timing."

Lawrence nods. "I didn't even know for sure that I was gay

until we'd been together for almost a year, to be honest. So, anyway, I tried to explain, but she threw me out. Didn't talk to me for weeks. She got quieter, shyer, . . . lonelier."

You broke her. Or she thinks you broke her, anyhow.

"But then why doesn't she just—" I stop midsentence. *Wish you straight?* is what I'm thinking, but I'm afraid to say it. I've never really spoken to the possible *subject* of a wish like this before. *Yes, Lawrence, I can manipulate you. Viola can wish, and I can change how you are.* I look away from him.

Lawrence shakes his head—he can see where I was going with that. "Not Viola—she won't. She's my best friend; she'd never wish to change me like that."

"But being with you would make her happy."

"Yeah, yeah. But it's not that easy. What a tangled web we weave, my friend," Lawrence says with a grin. "Just do me a favor and don't grant any stupid wishes for her."

Once a wish is made, I have to grant it, but I don't want to tell Lawrence that. He's not talking to me as a jinn, somehow. He's just talking to me. To *Jinn*. It's strange, and I'm not sure I want it to end by reminding him of protocol about respecting masters and wish rules. But doesn't he realize I'm just supposed to be a wish granter?

Lawrence takes a long sip of the beer he's holding. "Speaking of, can you see her in there? I don't want one of the football players to convince her to play beer pong or something."

I lean back on the railing and can just barely see the couch through the kitchen doors. But not Viola. She and Aaron are gone, leaving only an indentation and a few girls who look like they're withering into the cushions.

"She's gone. They're both gone—they were on the couch," I say with a grimace.

Lawrence sighs and wrinkles his brow in worry. "Help me find her?" he says. I nod. We go back inside, and Lawrence moves toward a dining room, where the table is covered in cards and shot glasses. I go in the opposite direction.

Masters and jinn are linked to each other, so usually I can find my master anywhere and reappear at her side. But right now, it's like the line between us is hidden by a thick fog. Though maybe it's because I'm trying to find her when it's not to grant a wish. I'm breaking the third protocol—helping her without a wish prevents me from getting back to Caliban as soon as possible. How many times have I broken all three protocol for her, now? I really shouldn't have pulled that stunt at the door, but they shouldn't have treated her like that. Like she didn't matter.

I don't see her anywhere on the lower floor, so I head for the staircase.

The upstairs is dark and cool, unlike the balmy lower floor. The music here is obscured, so all I can make out is the thudding bass, and the conversations that are so noisy downstairs are blurred into muted chatter. Every breath I take up here is loud, which is how I find her—the ragged sound of her breathing from the other end of the darkness.

"Viola?" I see her move in the black, and a feeling of relief crashes over me. "What are you doing?" I whisper. She's kneeling beside a door, fingers gripping the doorframe so hard, her knuckles are white. I look into the room that she's staring at, as if in a trance. Ollie and Aaron are locked in a tight embrace, Ollie mostly undressed and looking like some sort of ballerina or Roman goddess in the moonlight.

I turn back at Viola, and she breaks her gaze to look at me.

The deep wish, the wish to feel whole, looms in her eyes.

"They're so beautiful . . . see how they belong to each other?" she mumbles thickly. "I don't . . . I just don't . . . I didn't mean to watch. I just saw them and . . ." She releases the doorframe and shakily grabs my hand, then turns her face to me.

I hesitate.

I shouldn't help her without a wish. Third protocol. I should convince her to wish for belonging, right now, while she's desperate. Just like the Ancients demand. I should do everything in my power to return to Caliban as soon as possible.

I look back at Aaron and Ollie, then at Viola's eyes. She needs me. Me, not wishes, not a wish granter. Just me, just Jinn. No one has ever needed me, not like this. No one in Caliban needs anyone else. How could we need one another there, when we aren't even individual enough to have names?

Her hand is in mine. I turn her away from the door, resting her back against the wall and pulling her hair away from her lips. She pulls her knees to her chest, no hint of laughter or cleverness in her eyes. "You don't have to belong here, with these people," I say after a struggle for words.

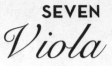

SEVEN

Viola

THE FOUR BEERS I drank are causing the hallway to sway and pitch. It's spinning even though I'm leaning against the wall, so I grab Jinn's shoulder to make it stop. He tenses, then leans closer to give me a better grip. I inhale the scent of honey and spices that always surrounds Jinn.

"I wasn't always so pathetic," I mumble. "I used to belong. I thought Lawrence and I would be one of those epic romances, the childhood friends who grow up loving each other and all that. Then one day, out of nowhere, he doesn't love me anymore. . . ." I close my eyes, and a few tears fall. "It was horrible. Suddenly there was no way I could ever, ever be what he wanted. No matter what—it didn't matter how I did my hair, or dressed, or smiled. I could never be what Lawrence wants. I can never have the epic romance. I can never have . . ." I let my words trail off.

I don't want to, but I can't help remembering the night Lawrence told me. My bedroom was shrouded in blue light, and the Flamingo Dream walls became a pale lavender that made everything look beautiful. Lawrence kissed me—my last real kiss—and I melted toward him and drew closer. Skin on skin, tingling closeness and lack of shame, and beauty and touching and love. And then? His words: *Wait. I have something to tell you.* And it was all over. And a part of me was ripped away.

Everyone else saw it coming, a voice in my head reminds me. *No one else was surprised.*

I exhale—I can smell the alcohol on my own breath— and shut my eyes. They knew. But I didn't. The same thoughts have been circling my mind daily since the moment Lawrence told me. Underneath those, however, lies another thought that scolds me.

Viola, you *knew from the start.*

You chose to see talking late at night, holding hands, fencing lessons, skin on skin, and lack of shame.

You closed your eyes to his sideways glances at boys, to the way that even when he kissed you, he didn't put his hands on you.

Because if I knew, then it's my fault.

It's your fault you're in pieces like this.

My stomach writhes, and I want to hold Jinn's hand and run from here, but my knees feel flimsy and weak—though if they're weak from the alcohol or from the memories, I'm not sure.

"I want to feel the way I used to feel when I was with Lawrence. I want to be whole again."

"You don't need him for that. You don't . . . you don't need anyone for that. You're already . . ." He looks away, then runs a hand through his hair nervously, like he's worried someone is watching. "You're already whole, and strong, and funny, and you don't need them." Suddenly I'm very aware of my right hand gripping Jinn's forearm and my left hand entwined with his fingers, aware of the fact that his skin is flawless and smooth and unlike anything I've ever touched. I bite at my lips, and my jaw trembles.

"Leave this house," Jinn says quietly, with an intense, penetrating stare, like he's reading from the back of my mind. "You don't need anyone here. I'll take you home."

Home. Away from these people, away from the only real social gathering I've been to in who knows how long. I shake my head. "But I just . . . I want to belong again. I want to be a part of something, so I can feel whole. Right now it's just . . ." I look back toward Ollie and Aaron. "I just wish I could belong like they do—" I stop.

My breath stops somewhere between my lungs and lips. *Wish*. I didn't mean to. Why am I so stupid? I release Jinn's arm, my heart pounding.

Jinn is watching me carefully, studying my face. He smiles but somehow looks sad. He rises with all the fluidity of a dancer and slowly pulls me up with him—when the hallway swirls, he locks his arms on my waist till I can meet his eyes again. What have I done? What did I wish for? I can't stop trembling. I try to tell Jinn to stop, but the words get lost in my throat.

Jinn exhales slowly and takes his hands off me, like he's

steadying a vase. He places one arm across his stomach, the other behind his back. He bows just a little, taking his dark eyes off me at the very last moment. Quietly, so quietly that I almost don't hear him, he speaks as he rises back to standing.

"As you wish."

EIGHT

Jinn

THE WISH PULLS at me like I'm standing in a rushing stream. I can shape the way it's granted, plunge my fingers into the water to make it flow the way I want. I grant it carefully, more meticulous than I've been in a long time. It would be easier to just let the wish flow through me and grant itself, but it might not be exactly what Viola had in mind; I want it to be right, not just the result of rushed, uncontrolled magic. I have to involve Aaron, unfortunately, and Ollie . . . all of them. I part the magic, let it flow together again. Even though I know it's just a mortal mind trick, I can't help hoping that I can grant the wish so she really will feel whole again. Maybe I can make her whole.

And then it's done. All laid out perfectly, like a rosebud flowering into flawless, symmetrical blossoms. I hear Aaron in the bedroom, telling Ollie he needs to leave, the rustling of clothes. Viola looks at me, and her watery eyes dry and fill with the same spark they have when she laughs—I'm instantly glad I included that spark in the granting of the wish. I want to watch her change, watch her sadness fall away, but I know that Aaron will come sweeping out of the bedroom at any moment and . . . no.

I vanish from the hallway—the magic will take care of everything now—and reappear in Holly Park. I collapse beneath the oak tree, staring into its branches at the night sky beyond. Maybe I should have stayed to make sure it all went as planned. Or to tell Lawrence about it. Or *something*.

No. Nothing.

I force my fingers into the dirt, as if I'm growing roots to hold me in place. She's my master, she made a wish. Nothing more to it.

Think of Caliban. Every wish gets you closer to Caliban. That's what's important. Not whether she thinks of you as a wish granter or not.

Think of all the things wrong with humans. The aging. That party. The way they're always answering phones. Microwave food. Dogs in shirts.

The way Viola laughs differently around you, the way she's not afraid to tell you off—

No, stop. Dogs in shirts. You're just a jinn—if you weren't granting Viola's wishes, it'd be some other random jinn. You're not special. She's not different around you.

"One wish in three days? It's your worst record yet!" a voice calls out through the early morning fog. I leap from the dirt, my heart racing in surprise.

Another jinn, a tall, golden-skinned boy with copper hair and bronze eyes, is standing beside the oak tree. I breathe a sigh of relief—he's a friend. Sort of. As good a friend as jinn typically have, anyway, though I'll admit that knowing Viola and Lawrence has redefined the term for me—they care for each other far more than this other jinn cares for me, I'm sure.

"Still better than your record was," I respond. I push him jokingly, and we both laugh. It's good to see one of my own kind again.

"Yeah, yeah. How are things?"

"Are you asking me as an ifrit or a friend?" I ask. He's wearing his work uniform, a dark blue tunic with a swirly *I* embroidered on the front. He's aged—a lot. The ifrit come and go between Caliban and Earth more often than average jinn do—whenever a press is needed—and the aging has started to show on his face. The boy—the *man*, actually, since he must be physically over twenty—laughs.

"You should have become an ifrit, my friend, and you wouldn't be stuck here granting wishes to begin with!" he says, dodging my question.

I nod and force a smile. Maybe he's right. The Ancient Jinn wanted me to be an ifrit once, not too long ago. I read mortals especially well, better than most jinn. So pressing came easily for me; I could tell exactly what would make the master snap, exactly what buttons to press to force him to wish.

"It wasn't for me," I answer, hoping to change the subject.

My brief stint in ifrit training isn't something I enjoy reflecting upon.

The ifrit laughs and shakes his head. "All because you couldn't complete a simple car wreck press."

"What can I say? I'm a wimp," I reply with a steely look. I hate it when people bring that up.

The ifrit realizes he's pushed too far and holds his hands up. "Sorry, my friend. Didn't mean to offend you."

"Right," I say, shaking my head. "Don't worry about it."

"Well, let me know if you need me to press her for the last two," the ifrit says.

"No! No . . . I don't need a press," I answer fast as my throat suddenly dries. The idea of Viola in a car wreck makes every muscle in my body tighten.

The ifrit shrugs. "Right. Anyway. I've got to go. There's a housewife in England trying to hold off on wishing. Thinks the jinn will crack and give her more wishes if she does."

I roll my eyes and relax a little. "Where do they get these ideas? I'll see you later. Don't worry about it—Viola will wish."

The ifrit, who had just turned on his heel to vanish, spins back around in a whirl of royal-blue silk, an eyebrow raised.

Damn.

"'Viola'?"

There's no way out of this, is there?

He's a friend. He won't care about the protocol. He won't report me to the Ancients. It'll be fine.

"My master. She insisted I call her by her first name," I explain. Can he tell that I *like* knowing her as *Viola* instead of *master*?

"But still . . . wow. Be careful violating the first protocol like that. The rules are in place for our own protection, you remember."

"Of course. You know teenage girls, though. They're not the easiest masters. Besides, you're one to talk about protocol." I grin to distract him.

The ifrit laughs. "Just because they don't monitor protocol for ifrit doesn't mean I don't try to follow the rules. It'd be impossible to complete some presses without breaking them."

"Excuses, excuses," I say.

"Yeah, yeah. Well, so long, my friend," he says. I nod in return, and the ifrit vanishes.

I exhale in relief—what if he'd asked why I don't want to press her? I would have had to . . . lie? Admit the truth? Punch him in the nose?

Wait. Why *don't* I want him to press her? She's just my master. Just the person whose wishes I happen to be granting. We've known each other only a few days. Yet something about the idea of her being pressed makes my muscles tense and my stomach flip.

Think of Caliban. This never happens in Caliban. No one ever makes you feel this way there. The Ancients make sure of it. You're one step closer to going home and leaving all this weirdness behind.

I sigh and drop to the ground, leaning against the oak tree. One step closer.

NINE

SOMETHING IS DIFFERENT.

The hallway isn't spinning. Jinn is gone—I grope for his arm in the dim light. I'm sitting on the floor. But it's something else, too. Like I've just woken up from a nap, only while I slept all my worries and concerns and fears fell away. Now I feel refreshed, and there's a shiny, almost crystalline feeling in my chest that makes me certain I can do *anything*—

"Viola?"

I turn around—the name doesn't sound normal, not at all the way it sounds when Jinn or Lawrence say it. Then I see why.

Aaron Moor is standing beside me, looking down at me with a confused smile.

"What are you doing?" he asks, raising an eyebrow.

He reaches down and pulls me up so fast that I get dizzy, then wraps an arm tightly around my waist. I lock my knees and try not to breathe. Surely this is a mistake. It's dark. He thinks I'm somebody else.

"Viola. I'm Vi—" I swallow my breath midsentence. I know what's different.

I wished. I wished to belong, like Aaron and Ollie.

"No . . . I didn't mean to . . . ," I begin, but the feeling of dread I'm anticipating never comes. Instead, I feel . . . happy. Relieved, even. Aaron swipes my hair from my eyes and grins at me.

"Come on," he says. "Let's go back downstairs—I wanted to introduce you to some people."

"What?"

"Some friends of mine—I don't know if you know them." Aaron studies me for a moment—I'm sure my mouth is hanging open. "You look amazing, by the way. I can't believe I didn't notice sooner. I guess I was too preoccupied with Ollie. . . . Not anymore though—we broke up. How could I stay with her when there's someone as beautiful as you here?" he finishes with a gentle grin.

I look beautiful. I look beautiful? I feel . . . I *feel* beautiful. And carefree, and reckless, and confident, and all the other things I felt before Lawrence, only more so. Aaron lets go of my waist, takes my hand in his, and walks forward—I stumble to follow him down the steps and into the living room, where the main party is still raging. Some part of me wants to drop my head in shyness, but some greater power forces me to keep my chin high, my shoulders back, my hand firmly in Aaron's. If arriving to the party before was like showing up to a Hollywood premiere, walking downstairs is now like being a red-carpet starlet, all kind smiles and people calling my name.

Aaron shouts for the music to change, and in the shuffle to switch CDs, people rise to grab drinks and new seats. Aaron and I—*Aaron and I?*—sit down together on a loveseat toward the front door. Girls I don't know walk over to us, asking me about my hair and clothes and if I hate Shakespeare as much as they do. All without wondering what my name is. As if they've always known me. As if I've always hung out with them. As if I've always belonged with them. Is this real?

I should feel guilty. This isn't natural. It isn't real. It's a *wish*.

But I don't feel guilty, not at all. I'm too happy. If I'd known how wonderful a single wish would make me feel, how much pain it could erase . . .

A new song thuds through the speaker system, and Aaron puts an arm around my shoulder, twirling his fingers through my hair in a way that makes shivers race down my spine. I want to lean in closer to him, but part of me is still reeling in fear that one false move will end everything. I catch Aaron's gaze—even the simple act of his eyes meeting mine makes me feel like I belong, like I suddenly warrant eye contact and conversation and meaningful glances instead of passing hallway nods. Like I'm special.

"What's going on?"

Lawrence. My eyes snap away from Aaron to see Lawrence standing beside the loveseat, arms folded. He doesn't look angry, just confused, eyes darting back and forth between Aaron and me.

"Not a lot, not a lot. Having a good time, though?" Aaron answers Lawrence. Lawrence nods curtly, and his eyes return heavily to mine. Two football players crash through the front door holding a keg. While Aaron is distracted cheering them on, I answer.

"I wished." I meant to speak the words aloud, but I only mouth them, afraid that saying it will somehow jinx things.

"You wished? For Aaron to date you? *That's* what you wished for?" Lawrence says, loud enough that I cringe and worry someone has heard. I grab Lawrence's hand and pull him closer.

"No! It was an accident; I didn't even *mean* to wish, it just slipped out. I wished to belong, like Aaron and Ollie, and then . . . I'm here! I don't know how, but it's . . . I feel . . ." How can I explain? I feel right. I feel this is where I belong, like I'm not alone.

"But it isn't real! It's just . . . it's just a wish, Viola! How could you wish for . . . for him?" Lawrence sounds hurt, betrayed even, and takes both my hands in his. "I know I hurt you, but this isn't the way to fix it."

"Then what is?" I answer. "Nothing in seven months has fixed me, but now . . . it's like all that unhappiness is just a memory. It isn't . . . it isn't *in* me anymore. I'm too happy for it to be in me."

"I want you to be happy because of who you are, Vi. Not because you wished for it."

"But until that happens," I say, casting a quick look at Aaron, "this is enough. Look at me, Lawrence. You can read me better than anyone. Please. I haven't felt like this in so long, like I belong—like I have more than just you and Jinn. Don't ruin this for me, Lawrence. You owe me." I've never called him out on the whole thing like that before, and to be honest, I'm not sure it's deserved.

Lawrence winces like I've struck him, then shakes his head. "I owe you? You know I didn't mean to hurt you."

"But it happened," I murmur. Lawrence sighs and squeezes my hand.

"I don't like it. But if this is what makes you happy—for now—then . . . fine. Fine." He looks defeated, but any guilt

I have is short-lived; it's like no unhappiness can exist in me right now. He releases my hands and glances around the room. "Where is Jinn, anyway?"

"He left," I answer. I dare to lean a little closer to Aaron, though I still don't think I can exactly fall into his arms. "Right after the wish. He helped me to the floor and then . . . left."

"Who?" Aaron asks, floating back into our conversation.

"No one," Lawrence answers before I can stammer a reply. He looks back at me, a forced calm on his face. "We're still getting breakfast before I drop you off at home, right?"

We had no such plans, and to be honest, I'm afraid to leave—what if leaving the party makes the wish end? I can't go back to being an Invisible Girl. Not again. Still, Lawrence is . . . well, Lawrence. I nod and lean in closer to Aaron as Lawrence vanishes into the crowd.

TEN

Jinn

"JINN!"

It isn't Viola calling my name—it's Lawrence. The sky is on the verge of lightening; the trees are silhouettes instead of just blackness. I rise from underneath the oak tree, brushing the dirt off my legs. So he's found out about the wish now, too. I could hide out here, not face him—I'm not bound to his call like I am to Viola's. But no . . . he deserves answers. I sigh, then vanish from the park to reappear beside him.

"Wow. Calling you actually worked," Lawrence says. He's sitting in the driver's seat of his car outside the party house. It's eerie, seeing the house that was thrashing with life only a few hours earlier—it's now quiet and calm, save for a few people staggering toward their cars. Morning dew covers the red cups strewn throughout the yard and has soaked through the clothing of a guy passed out underneath the front hedges.

"I'm waiting on Viola to come out. Get in the car," Lawrence says firmly, his initial surprise worn off. I nod, trying to gauge how angry he is about the wish, but he's difficult to read at the moment. I circle around the car and slide into the passenger seat, holding my hands to the vents to warm them.

"We need to talk," Lawrence says, giving me a hard look.

I sigh. "Look, she wished. I *had* to. I didn't want to, to be honest."

"I'm not mad. But I want to know exactly how it works. I mean, say Viola wants to leave him . . . will he still love her?"

I shake my head. "Sort of. Not really. Wishes aren't permanent. She wished for what Aaron and Ollie had, so . . . I made him want her instead of Ollie. It was the best way to give her what she wanted without changing too much about who *she* is. Anyway, I tweaked the wish here and there. I did what I could. I tried to turn it into a wish to belong, not a wish for love. But it can end, just like anything else."

"Okay . . . okay. Good." Lawrence looks slightly relieved.

"And I left you out of it. Nothing about you changed," I add. Letting the magic touch Lawrence just didn't seem right.

Lawrence looks back over at me, sighing and shaking his head. "Um . . . thanks? You know, you and your wishes really don't make any of this easier."

I muster a weak smile. "'What a tangled web we weave,' right?"

"Something like that," Lawrence replies, rubbing his temples. We both turn to look when movement from the front of the house catches our eyes. It's Viola, walking slowly through the front door, hand in hand with Aaron. They're followed by a small group of Aaron's friends, who don't look nearly as glamorous in the dawn light as they did the last time I saw them. Viola, however, glows brightly. Aaron pulls her close, and she lifts her shoulders shyly, then gives a bubbly laugh and gives in to his touch.

Aaron and Viola approach my door and stop. I meet Viola's eyes briefly before they disappear behind Aaron's head as he moves in to kiss her. Lawrence and I busy ourselves by hitting the car radio buttons. Repeatedly. Finally, Aaron releases her and opens the passenger door; I dive to the backseat.

"Hey, Lawrence, where'd you disappear to?" Aaron asks, grinning and rubbing his hands against the morning chill.

"Just came out here for a while," Lawrence answers dully as Viola buckles her seatbelt. She glances back at me and gives me a small smile.

"See you tomorrow morning, baby," Aaron says, and closes the car door.

No one speaks. Viola keeps biting her lips and giving both Lawrence and me nervous glances. There's a wish in her eyes—to tell us about the rest of her evening.

Thanks, but no thanks. "Where are we going?" I ask Lawrence to avoid continuing the awkward silence.

"Breakfast. Or an extremely late dinner," he says, motioning toward the clock—it's five fifteen in the morning.

"I've never been awake this early before," Viola comments. "Or I guess I've never really been out this late before. Time just flew, I was sitting with Aaron, and then we danced—"

"*You* danced?" Lawrence says, sounding surprised.

"I know! Aaron made me do it, but then it was kind of fun, and then we sat outside until it got really cold....You were out here in the car? And where were you, Jinn?"

Lawrence nods while I answer aloud, "Holly Park. I go there at night. If you close your eyes . . . and your ears . . . and try not to inhale, it's a little like Caliban. Sort of."

Viola turns around in her seat to look at me. "Caliban— which, may I add, you're closer to, now that I've wished." As soon as she says it her grin fades a little, to less of a beam and more of a reluctant smile.

"That's right, just two more wishes," I reply and force myself to think of what I'd be getting for breakfast were I in Caliban. Food is taken seriously there. It's all elegantly prepared and served, perfectly garnished—

"I hope they still serve that Bacon Breakfast plate," Lawrence says, swinging the car off the road and into the parking lot of a small, dirty-looking breakfast joint.

The restaurant is packed with all sorts—silent brooders, chatty teenagers, and the occasional leering old man. It smells like stale smoke and bacon inside, and the waitresses shout orders to a large cook who shuffles back and forth in front of the stovetop, frying eggs and pouring waffle batter. We slide into a booth, Lawrence on one side and Viola and I on the other. I fixate on watching the cook in disgust in order to avoid hearing Viola's stories about the great Aaron Moor.

Think of Caliban. The view from my apartment. Delivering flowers. The curved architecture, the street fairs, the wildflowers . . .

"It helps if you don't watch him cook," Lawrence says from across the booth.

"What?" I ask, snapping back to reality.

"The cook. It helps if you don't actually watch him make the food. You're starting to look sort of sick."

"He's right, Jinn. Do you want some of this toast?" Viola asks. She slides her plate toward me until our elbows bump briefly.

I shake my head. "I'm fine. Sorry. I don't need food on Earth, remember?" The jukebox kicks on an annoying song about waffles, for which most of the customers cheer.

"I hate this song," Lawrence groans, hitting his head on the table.

"Anyway," Viola says, ignoring Lawrence and meeting my eyes, "I never thanked you, Jinn. For helping me, I mean."

"Don't worry about it. You wished, I didn't really have a choice anyhow—"

"I meant before that," Viola cuts me off with a meaningful look. The hall, I realize. With Aaron and Ollie, when I pulled her away and she grabbed for my arm . . . when I was her friend, not her wish granter.

"I see how it is. Suddenly Viola and her genie-boy have secrets," Lawrence says, waving a syrup-covered fork at me. Viola laughs again—deep, real laughter that's brighter than the repetitive waffle song. I finally smile—the first time since her wish, I think. It's hard to feel regretful when she's laughing.

ELEVEN

AARON MEETS ME in the cafeteria on Monday morning, throwing an arm around my shoulder and handing me a paper cup of cappuccino. He ushers me over to a table where some of the Royal Family is sitting; a girl compliments my jacket, and another invites me to a movie this weekend. I'm sure I'm grinning and giggling like an idiot, but I can't really help myself.

"She's in the Art Expo thing," Aaron says, giving me an admiring look.

"Really? Is that hard? Painting and drawing?" a girl asks me as she shuffles through her purse for lipstick. Damn. I should have worn lipstick—Ollie always wears lipstick. I scan the cafeteria for her golden skin, both hoping and fearful that I'll see her. I wonder if she's furious with me for stealing her throne. A swell of guilt courses through me at the thought that I haven't seen her since the party, since the wish—

"Viola?" the lipstick girl interrupts my thoughts. I snap back into the conversation.

"It's . . . ah," I stammer. Somehow telling these people that painting is about being passionate just doesn't sound right. "It's hard to know if you've done something well or not. After a while you start to see only its problems."

A few people nod; Aaron kisses my hand. "Speaking of painting," he adds, "can a few of you guys help me this afternoon with the *Grease* sets? I was supposed to do them Sunday, but I was *way* too hung over to handle it." A few friends nod and volunteer.

"I can't," I say, feeling a little guilty. "I need to work on my Expo paintings, actually. I slept all day Sunday and didn't get a chance to come in."

Aaron shakes his head. "Don't worry about it, baby." He

kisses me—this time on the mouth—before I have a chance to think. My cheeks burn bright red—there are *so* many people around, and I'm not certain if I'm more proud to be kissing Aaron or embarrassed that everyone is watching. What if they're wondering what Aaron Moor is doing with a girl like me? What if they know it's because of a wish? Aaron presses hard into my mouth until I close my lips and pull my head away. Aaron grins and runs his thumb over my hands. "Sorry. Got carried away." The rest of the table laughs before launching into a conversation about hangover cures.

Still flustered and scarlet from the kiss, I keep quiet, pretending to be interested in a girl walking up to each table in the cafeteria. She's carrying a blue cardboard box that reads "FUNdraiser" on the side. She belongs to the band kids, I think. The girl meets my eyes and heads my way.

I don't know her name. She doesn't fit in with the Royal Family; her eyebrows are ungroomed and her clothes aren't ridiculously tight. Yet even so, she doesn't look intimidated or even nervous about approaching the table. Instead, she looks defeated, like she's already anticipating being ignored or passed over.

"Hi. The marching band is selling candy to go to Philadelphia. One dollar per bar, anyone interested?"

No one hears her—no one but me, anyhow. The Royal Family continues chattering without looking up. As if she's invisible. She sighs and scouts out another table.

"Wait," I say, just as she's about to step away from the table. The girl raises her eyebrows at me; does she remember that I was just like her only a few days ago? Or did Jinn change that as well?

"I'll take two," I say, digging through my purse for two dollars bills. I hand them over and take two packs of Skittles from the blue cardboard box.

"Ooo, candy!" a Royal Family girl says from the end of the table.

"What are you selling it for?" one of the guys says, throwing a dollar into the box and grabbing a Twix. The band girl rolls her eyes a little, and I can't help snickering. She repeats the spiel and, when she's finished, gives me a sort of grateful nod. I return the nod and look away only to see Jinn watching me, leaning against the trophy case with a sort of satisfied smile. I raise an eyebrow at him, and he shrugs, then vanishes.

When I arrive at the art room after the last bell, I head straight for the pink paint. And violet. And orange. Somehow I feel like I can paint with all of them, can splash color on the canvas and be carefree about it all. I shove my old paintings aside and pull up a new sheet of canvas, not even caring when my fingers accidently smear paint on the clean edges. I step back and look at the blank space.

But what to paint? There's so much that's shiny and sparkly and would lend itself to an amazing piece of art. I press my lips together.

"Paint a picture of me being bored at a park for the last eight hours," Jinn says. I turn and grin at him.

"I couldn't do you justice, sir," I reply. "Besides, you were here this morning, so it wasn't really eight hours."

"Fair," Jinn says, stealing the remaining pack of Skittles from my purse. "I just wanted to make sure things are going okay."

"They are. Things are going great, actually." Jinn lifts himself onto a table while I turn back to the canvas. "Though I have to admit, I thought painting would be easier. I mean, I know I want to use these colors, but . . . wow. Painter's block."

"Wait . . . ," Jinn says. He steps up behind me and takes the paintbrush from my hand. "I've got it. It'll be brilliant." He dips the end of the paintbrush in crimson paint and slowly paints a smiley face in the center of the canvas.

I laugh, but Jinn steps back and folds his arms, admiring his work, before motioning for me to have a shot at the picture. I rinse the brush and dip it in fuchsia, then add spiky hair to the face. I pause as the paint dries—it looks sort of like the Punk Guy from my Shakespeare class. I didn't think about sketching him today, like I usually do. Didn't even occur to me.

"Viola?" Jinn says when I haven't spoken for a few moments.

"Sorry," I say, turning to him. "Your turn?"

He shakes his head. "Nope. You can't add to perfection."

"Naturally," I answer. I'm about to continue when I hear footsteps approaching the art room. Aaron appears in the doorway.

"Hey, baby," he says, eyes sparkling. He looks at the smiley face painting as he walks toward me. "That's . . . um . . ."

I blush. "We—I—was just playing around."

"Hey! That was serious art," Jinn says behind me.

"Well, it's magnificent," Aaron teases me. He kisses my cheek and entwines his fingers with mine, while I try to avoid touching his clothes with my wet paintbrush. Aaron is warm and inviting, but I'm very, very aware of Jinn's dark eyes on me.

"Great," Jinn says with a look of resignation. "Another four hours sitting in a park."

Sorry, I mouth. He sighs, but gives me a wry smile before he vanishes.

Aaron wraps an arm around my waist. "Come on," he says, and steps toward the door, pulling my hand with him.

"Wait," I say, motioning toward the painting. "I really need to work on the Expo stuff. . . ." Aaron runs a hand across my back. It sends a pleasant shiver through me.

"I need to put my stuff away at least," I half-heartedly protest.

Aaron raises an eyebrow. "Put it away later. I have something to show you."

I bite my lip, and he leans in to kiss my forehead. He slides one hand down my arm and gently plucks the wet paintbrush from my fingers, dropping it onto the counter. I should put it in water—it'll ruin the brush, leaving it out to dry too long. Aaron pulls me toward the door.

The halls are empty of everything but the sounds of teachers complaining in the break room and the whir of the janitors' vacuums. Aaron stops just as we reach the theater doors.

"Wait just a second," he says, and reaches into his back pocket. He pulls out a shred of cloth that I'm pretty sure was ripped from the school's Juliet costume.

"You've got to be kidding," I say through a smile as he moves to tie it around my eyes.

"You know, you don't make it easy for a guy to be romantic," Aaron answers. I laugh and give in. Awkward or not, who am I to turn down a romantic gesture?

Aaron puts his hands on my shoulders and leads me into the cool theater. It smells like spray paint and mildew, and I can hear my steps echoing as we walk. Aaron navigates me up the wing stairs and onto the stage.

"Ready?" he asks.

"Yes," I say, a little breathless.

Aaron sweeps the blindfold off my eyes. It's almost completely dark in the theater. In the blackness of the ceiling, tiny glowing lights appear, fake stars that haven't been used in a show for ages. Aaron nods toward the lighting booth, where a few of his friends are hanging out. They give him a thumbs-up, then hit the stage lights, illuminating Aaron and me in a pale blue-violet glow.

"Get it? Like it's nighttime?" Aaron says, motioning at the stars above.

I nod and give as girlish a laugh as I can muster. Aaron turns around to where a blanket is spread out in the center of the stage, with a Gatorade bottle and a bag of miniature Snickers beside it.

"I got bored painting *Grease* sets, so I made us a picnic under the stars instead," Aaron says, looking pleased with himself. I grin so hard, it nearly hurts. He did this for me. Even

Lawrence never did anything like this for me.

Aaron and I sit down on the blanket, and he swigs from the Gatorade bottle—I can smell the beer inside that's replaced the actual Gatorade. He leans on the scaffolding that's right behind us, sweeping his hair back. I wonder where the rest of Aaron's friends are—I thought they always hung out together. It's a little strange, being with Aaron alone in an empty theater. I look up at the fake stars.

"You know, this sounds stupid, but I mean it when I say I had a great time with you Saturday," Aaron says, holding my gaze. I blush—I can feel my cheeks heating up—and nod in return. Aaron leans in and turns my face toward his. I struggle to swallow the mini Snickers I bit into just a moment before. Our lips touch.

Aaron's kiss is powerful, strong, like he might push me backward if I don't return it with just as much force. It makes my heart pump and my hands shake. I can smell his cologne; the scent is overpowering. Jinn would have something to say about a cologne bath, but I wouldn't blame him. I'll take the honey-spice scent of Jinn's skin over a bottle of Ralph Lauren any day. I wonder what he's doing, hanging out in a sketchy park. . . . I shouldn't have ditched him this afternoon.

I pull away from Aaron and smile. He grins and takes another swig of his drink.

"I can't stay out too late," I say after a moment's silence. I look up at the fake stars.

"Really? I wanted you to come over and watch a movie or something."

I press my lips together. "No, I want to, it's just . . ." I sip my drink to stall and give me a moment to think. I can't exactly say that I feel guilty about Jinn being alone. "Don't you have to finish the *Grease* sets today?"

Aaron laughs. "True, true. I just like spending time with you, I guess. But lame musicals wait for no one!"

When Aaron drops me off at home, it's already dusk outside. My mom looks up from starching a row of her white blouses as I walk in the door.

"And where were you?" she asks, eyeing Aaron's car as he drives away.

"I was . . . on a date, I guess," I say as I open the refrigerator and hunt for a can of Diet Coke.

"A date?" my mom says, her voice an odd mix of doubt and relief. She sprays down the closest shirt with the can of starch. "You didn't tell me you had a date. With whom? Or was it Lawrence?"

"No!" I snap, defensively enough that my mom rolls her eyes. "It was with Aaron Moor. He's from school. Did you want me to start telling you that sort of thing?"

"Oh, no, it's okay. I was just wondering," my mom says. She pauses for a moment, a thoughtful look on her face, then sets the can of spray starch down. "He's nice, then?"

I nod. Relationship talk is not something my parents and I are good at.

"Good, good." She crunches the sleeve of a blouse as I open my drink and begin to head to my room. "Viola," she calls out after me. She leans against the kitchen table. "I don't need to worry about you or anything, right? We can have the talks if you want."

"The talks?"

She furrows her eyebrows and shrugs. "You know . . . sex

talk. Drinking talk. Love talk. We've never had them. Just don't think I'm too busy with work for the talks if you need them. I think I can order a DVD about teenage sexuality. I guess I should have done it while you were with Lawrence but . . . better late than never, right?"

If there's one phrase I never want to hear my mom say again, it's *teenage sexuality*. I want to burst out laughing, but my mom seems so perplexed and sincere that I can't bring myself to embarrass her. Instead I shake my head furiously as I open my bedroom door. "I'm good, Mom. But I'll let you know if I need any talks."

"Talks?" Jinn says as I shut the door behind me. He's leaning against the wall by the window, arms folded, with an amused smirk on his face.

"Sex talks," I say with a grin. "Apparently there's even a DVD."

"You, Aaron, and your mom should probably watch that together. You know, educational experience," he replies with a serious expression. I throw a pillow at him, which he dodges at the last moment.

"So how was the hot date?" he says as I lay back on my bed and inhale the scent of old quilts.

I smile. "It was . . . strange. And it was great."

"Right," he replies so quickly that it's clear he doesn't want to hear the gritty details of my afternoon. Jinn runs a hand through his hair several times, paying close attention to the moment the hair slips from his fingers.

"Four days," Jinn says under his breath. I sit up and look at him. "I've been here four days."

"That doesn't seem right," I reply, tallying numbers in my head. "It feels like you've been here weeks."

Jinn rolls his eyes like he's annoyed, but his voice is soft. "It just seems like longer because we've spent so much time together." He runs his hand through his hair again. "My hair has grown. A lot. Four days is a long time if you're not used to aging."

"Four days . . . only four days." I don't even like saying it. I watch him finger his hair again. We both smile.

TWELVE

Jinn

"I CAN CUT it," Viola says from the nest of quilts, a sly look in her eyes.

I laugh. "No amount of wishing is going to convince me to let you anywhere near my head with a pair of scissors."

"No, I'm serious! I used to cut Lawrence's."

"I don't care if you cut Keanu's hair, stay away from me," I say, folding my arms over my chest.

"No? Fine. Then . . . I guess you want to hear all about my afternoon with Aaron . . . ," she begins carefully.

"Not especially."

"Oh no, it was wonderful. I'll be sure to go into all the

119

sappy details. . . . I mean, it's just as well you don't trust me enough to cut your hair, because if you did, I'd be too busy focusing to talk, but—"

"You can really cut hair? Promise?" I'm not sure I can stomach another few hours of her talking about Aaron. Over breakfast was enough.

"I wouldn't offer if I was going to butcher your head. Really. If the length is bothering you, let me cut it."

I study her carefully. Her eyes are pleading, her lips curved in a small smile and her fingers, I can tell, itching for scissors.

If we aren't supposed to call our masters by their first names, I'm pretty sure haircutting is out of the question. But I sigh and nod. I'm pretty desperate not to hear the details of her date with Aaron.

Viola motions toward her desk chair, then sweeps a blanket on the floor around it. I sit down as she shuffles around in her bathroom, emerging with a pair of silver scissors. She snaps them at me and laughs.

"I'm having second thoughts."

"Aaron and I kissed—"

"Cut away," I say, holding up my hands in defeat. She leans on her desk behind me, wiping the scissors down with a wet cloth.

"I told you, relax. I really do know how to do this. Well, enough for a guy anyhow."

"That's not especially reassuring. Somehow I don't believe that a sixteen-year-old can cut hair."

"Well, do *you* know how?"

"No. But our hair doesn't grow in Caliban—"

"Yeah, yeah. And how old are you?" she asks, stepping around to the front of my chair.

"A hundred and seven," I answer.

Viola raises her eyebrows but laughs. "Then you're overdue anyhow. How short is it supposed to be?" She sits down on the bed, ours knees inches apart, and watches as I pull the hair on my forehead straight.

"It's hard to remember, actually." I can't believe it's hard to remember four days ago. "I think maybe to here?" I say, placing my forefinger where I'm guessing my hair should be. She nods and rises, moving behind me and out of sight. There's a strange pause, and then she pulls her fingers through my hair. She smiles—I'm not sure how, but I can tell she's smiling—and I relax back into the chair.

"It can't seriously have grown that much in four days," she says, running her fingers through a second time. Her fingertips feel like flower petals, and she spirals them down around the nape of my neck.

"It grows faster when we're here, like it's catching up or something. Four days' worth is a lot."

Viola steps in front of me again, and bends down so her face is even with mine. I know she's actually looking at my hair, but it looks like she's looking straight at me—I close my eyes to avoid the stare.

"Okay," she says, pinching the hair by my temples between her fingers. "Ready?"

"You've got scissors near my head. I don't have a choice."

"This is true," Viola says, and I can hear the grin in her voice. The scissors swish and click sharply right by my ear. I open my eyes just a crack to see the black curl in Viola's palm. "That wasn't so terrible, right? Now hold still—"

"Stop," I say, staring at four days' difference in her hand. If she cuts it all off, what do I have to even show that I've been here? It'll be like she never summoned me.

Viola looks from the cut she's about to make to my eyes. "I told you, you can trust me!" she says, sounding both amused and exasperated.

"No, no." I lean away from the scissors. "It's just . . . I don't know. I've never had long hair. Er—longer hair. Maybe I'll see how it goes before I let you hack away at it," I tease. Viola smiles and drops the scissors on her desk.

"Then I guess I get to go into detail about my afternoon without you?"

"Please, no," I say. I'm smiling, it sounds light, but the truth is, there's nothing I want to hear about less than how the wish is working on Viola.

"Fine, fine, I'll spare you for now. But I'm going to a movie with him tomorrow. You're going to have to hear the details one way or another. Unless I get drunk again and make two more wishes and you leave," she says, grinning at her own joke.

"Eh, I'm sort of used to you not wishing," I reply quietly.

The idea of her and Aaron alone in a theater darkens my mood. His hands on her, the way he looks at her hungrily . . . it's disturbing. I shake the image from my mind. "I should go, I guess. For the night, I mean."

Viola shrugs, and her cheeks turn a little bit pink. "You don't have to go now, unless you want to. I mean . . . I don't want you to watch me sleep or anything. That's weird. But you don't have to leave altogether."

I lean back in the chair, balancing it against the edge of the desk. "We'll see. I like the park at night. And I don't know about sitting in this chair for eight hours."

"Hey! That's a great chair," she says, smiling as she tosses her quilts back and climbs into the bed. She studies me for a moment before reaching over and pulling the chain on her bedside lamp, casting the room in darkness. The air conditioner kicks on, billowing her curtains back just enough that I see a glimpse of the stars outside.

"I have a question," she says, her voice a little muffled from the blankets.

"Yes?" I reply, rising and going to the window. I part the

curtains and look at the stars.

"Are you happy here?"

I'd expected some question about Aaron and wish mechanics or something, so her words startle me. I close the curtains and turn toward her.

"I . . . why?" I stumble on my words. The question tugs at me gently, but I can feel her good intentions: She's giving me the choice not to answer.

Viola sits up, pulling the blankets to her chest and avoiding my eyes. "I just . . . you're my friend. If you're still miserable here, I'll make two more wishes so you can go back," she says, trying to mask the reluctance in her voice.

It's that simple. Right now, she'll wish.

"No," I reply.

"Oh. Okay, then I'll just wish—"

"No!" I cut her off sharply. "I mean, don't wish. I don't mind being here, staying until you decide what you really want. They're your wishes; you should take your time. Caliban isn't going anywhere." I sit down in the armchair.

I just said that. I just turned wishes down.

"Good," she says, and lays back down. "I just . . . I'd miss . . ."
She trails off and her cheeks flush bright red. She picks at the
loose threads in her quilt. "Anyhow. So what's Caliban like?"
she asks quickly.

I smile and let my head rest against the back of the armchair. "I don't know. It's still. Everything is very still, compared
to here."

"Boring?" Viola asks.

"No, not boring. I just mean . . . no one ages. No one hurries. No one gets excited about Art Expos or dates or whatever,
because . . . well, you have a lifetime for that sort of thing."

"What does it look like, though?" Viola replies.

"It's like . . . you know how before they build a new sky-
scraper or apartments, they put up a picture of the building
surrounded by trees and flowers and everything?"

"Yeah—only it never ends up being surrounded by much
more than concrete."

"But in Caliban, it is. You have the giant glass buildings
but then . . . the flowers."

"It sounds like Oz," she says. "Like in the movies, I mean, with the Emerald City. . . ." As she drifts off, I'm suddenly very aware that she's looking at me. Our eyes lock for a long time. "You're sure you want this place instead of a fancy city garden?" she adds.

I exhale and nod. "This place has its charms, too. You don't have the Ancients breathing down your neck here, talking about repopulating Caliban and all that. You want to hear some sex talks. . . ."

Viola laughs, and though I can't see her face, I know it's lit up in the shadows. "Repopulate? So wait, you said there are only a few thousand jinn, right?"

"Give or take, I imagine."

"Why so few?"

I run my hands along the chair arms for a moment, enjoying the rippling of fabric beneath my fingers. "Well, if you believe the Ancients, it's all part of our punishment."

"Punishment?"

My eyes are growing used to the darkness, and I can just

make out the outline of her form, sitting up and hugging her knees in bed.

"It's this old story, sort of like our own little creation tale. The myth is that ages ago, jinn and humans lived here together. Jinn had magical powers, but instead of using them for the good of everyone—human and jinn alike—they used it for personal gain, power, selfishness, that sort of thing. So as punishment, jinn were made the servants of wishing humans and banished to Caliban."

"It doesn't sound like it's a terrible place to be banished to."

"I never figured out that part either, to be honest. But keep in mind, that part is all just a myth. The only hard facts are that as the population here grows, more and more people have wishes. Eventually there were too many mortals with wishes for the jinn to keep up with, so instead of everyone getting their wishes granted, the Ancients select a few hundred at a time—I think they try to spread out the wishes so you don't have too many people in one area suddenly winning the lottery or becoming rock stars. But the more often we're called, the more often we're here. The more often we're here, the more often we age. And the more often we age—"

"The more often you grow old and die," Viola finishes for me.

"Exactly," I answer, leaning forward to rest my elbows on my knees. "Combine that with the fact that we don't attach to one another like you people do, and you don't exactly have a recipe for a booming population. That's why there's all the protocol, all the rules, all the desperation to increase the population. The Ancients want us in, out, and back to our normal lives; they make our masters forget all about us so there's no risk they'll tell other humans that we exist and can be summoned. They're afraid that we'll die out."

"I don't want you to die," Viola says in a small voice.

My head jerks up. "No, no. Don't worry about that," I mumble quietly, as if I'm afraid the Ancients will hear me from Caliban.

"I'll wish if you want. Really."

"I told you, no. They're your wishes."

"Right," Viola sighs. "Well, let me know if you . . . if you change your mind. About me wishing now, I mean."

"Okay."

But I know I won't.

THIRTEEN

Viola

I GRUMBLE AND swat at my alarm. No matter how many times I've been late to school because of hitting the SNOOZE button, I know it's an unbreakable morning habit. The pop song blasting through the tiny speaker is silenced, and I prepare to fall back asleep for seven minutes. A soft laugh interrupts the quiet.

Jinn. I sit bolt upright in the bed, clutching the covers to my chest. Jinn is sitting in the arm chair, legs swung up over the side and arms folded.

"You stayed," I say, trying to cover my surprise.

"You abuse alarm clocks," he responds.

"Something like that," I answer, and try to smooth the tangled nest that is my hair. "Decided the park would be fine by itself for a night?" I kick my legs over the side of the bed—no point in trying to fall back asleep now.

"To be honest," Jinn says as I step into the bathroom and let the shower water heat up, "I forgot to leave. I was just watching stars and then . . . it was morning."

"The exciting life of a magical creature," I tease. Jinn rolls his eyes.

I shower quickly and dress in the bathroom; when I emerge, Jinn is flipping through old copies of *Seventeen* with a look of mild disgust.

"So, you're going to a movie with Aaron tonight? I imagine that means more park time for me?" Jinn asks, shutting the magazine and pushing it away.

"It's only a few hours," I explain. "We're not even going to dinner, just to see some horror movie or something."

"But you hate horror movies," Jinn replies. He says it in a matter-of-fact way that tells me he simply read it in my eyes— the wish not to see movie murders.

"I don't *hate* horror movies. I just . . . don't watch them," I say, opening and slamming drawers in an attempt to find a hairbrush.

"Why is he taking you to see a horror movie when you hate horror movies?" Jinn asks, studying my eyes and, I'm sure, reading my distaste for gore. I have to admit that I've sort of gotten used to him reading me. It's even nice, sometimes, to be able to explain everything with just a look. Jinn rises and grabs my hairbrush from under a stack of shirts, then hands it to me. I blush and nod in appreciation before I respond.

"It's not about the movie, it's about doing something together. That's the point of dates, you know, dark theaters and cuddling or whatever."

"Right," Jinn says, cringing. "Sounds . . . great. Really."

I laugh. "It's nice to feel attractive and . . . um . . . appreciated," I say, trying to be tactful.

Jinn grimaces. "Don't tell me about it," he says as I head downstairs. "I guess I'll see you after then?"

"Yes. I mean, unless you had big plans for the park?" I'm only half teasing; the idea of Jinn just waiting around for me to call him is a little uncomfortable, though I have to admit it's pleasant knowing he'll always be there when I want him to. He studies me for a moment, reading the concern in my eyes.

"No," he says, smiling. "No plans—and it's my job to be here when you need me, you know. Don't worry about it."

Jinn was right. I hate horror movies.

Even the poster I'm staring at freaks me out a little. I mean, how many of these *Saw* movies do they have to make before people get sick of watching teenage girls be tortured? I shiver even though it's not cold, and look longingly at a poster for a generic Meg Ryan comedy.

"I've got the tickets, baby," Aaron says from behind me. I tear my eyes away from the poster to see him holding two orange tickets and motioning to the theater door. Aaron wraps an arm around me and tugs me close to him as we enter, heading straight to theater twelve without stopping for snacks. It's probably for the better anyhow, since I'm not sure I could eat Twizzlers while someone's eyeball is melting on screen.

"I really think you'll like this," Aaron says as we find a

spot toward the back of the theater. "I mean, I don't think you'll be able to walk away from this and say you still hate horror movies."

"I doubt that," I mumble nervously. I can feel my cheeks burning pink—what kind of sixteen-year-old is afraid of a movie?

I sigh and sit back as the theater darkens and the previews begin. Aaron raises the armrest between us and kisses my forehead—it still makes me feel warm, even with the impending eyeball destruction. I force myself to think of things like forehead kisses, things that make me happy. How about the fact that, for once, I'm not sitting alone in the art room after school? That I'm on a date with Aaron Moor, my *boyfriend*? Better to be in a scary movie with someone who likes me than sitting at home alone. Well, not *alone* really. Since Jinn showed up, the whole sitting at home thing has been a little less painful. Still, I'm actually on a date. One melting eyeball scene is a fair trade for a social life, right?

Aaron slides a hand behind my lower back and lets it rest on my hip as the actual movie begins to roll. I try not to pay too much attention, since getting attached to the perky blonde starlet will probably ensure her horrible death. Aaron grins at me, then shakes his head at my obvious nervousness, pulling me closer. I turn my head to his shoulder and squeeze my eyes shut when a starlet is quietly offed, and the rest of the beautiful cast decides to split up and look for their missing friend. Mental note: Tell Lawrence and Jinn that if I ever go missing in a creepy house, don't bother looking for me.

"Baby, you're missing it," Aaron whispers to me.

"Good," I mutter back. Aaron laughs quietly and squeezes me. At least this is romantic, curling up beside Aaron . . . even if I'm doing so while the sounds of bones breaking shoots through the theater. It's hard not to yank my hands up and cover my ears.

"You're really scared, aren't you?" Aaron realizes.

"Told you I'm a wimp," I whisper back without removing my head from the folds of his shirt. Aaron chuckles and tilts my head toward his, then kisses me on the mouth. It's a slow kiss, deep, and I worry for a moment about the other moviegoers watching us. Not that anyone should be ashamed to be seen kissing Aaron Moor, but still, it makes me feel weird. I pull out of the kiss, returning my head to his shoulder.

Aaron laughs under his breath, then guides my face back to his, this time leaning in on me, blocking my view of the screen. I try to ignore the feeling of eyes on us and kiss him back. I pull away slightly, attempt to make it a little less passionate, but when Aaron presses harder against me, I give in.

FOURTEEN
Jinn

I CRINGE.

I can't watch this. I don't mean the abysmal movie that's playing—I mean Aaron practically on top of Viola. He brushes her hair aside and nuzzles her neck like they're in some sort of love hideaway instead of a half-full theater. I grit my teeth and touch the lock of hair by my temple, the single curl that's shorter from where Viola cut it. *Stop it,* I command myself. *They're just kissing. If you keep this up, she's going to realize you're here.*

Someone behind me tosses ice at them; it grazes across Viola's cheek, causing her to jerk back from Aaron's lips. She gives an apologetic glance to the guy who threw the ice, looking right through me as I sit invisible in the row behind her. Even though I know she can't see me, I freeze, afraid to be caught; not so much because this breaks the first protocol about respecting her, but rather because I know she'll be furious with me. But I couldn't stand the thought of her and Aaron here alone, especially not after the wishes I saw in Aaron's eyes when he picked her up . . . wishes that mostly involve scenes straight out of Playboy. I shiver. *She's not yours to protect,* I chant to myself. It doesn't help.

The wishes in Viola's eyes are nothing like Aaron's—she wishes to be watching a comedy, to be cuddling with Aaron on her living room couch, to be painting. She doesn't want to be here. And the public makeout session in the middle of a gory movie in a sticky-floored theater? Can't Aaron read her wishes at *all*? I should've included that ability when I made him love her.

I sigh. *Tell him no, Viola. This isn't what you want.*

Viola doesn't speak. Aaron smiles, then kisses her again.

Tell him no!

Viola kisses Aaron back, and I clench my fists. *Don't give in like this just because he loves you!* Aaron's hand slips down and runs up Viola's thigh.

I should leave. I shouldn't be here. I'm just a wish granter! I shouldn't have any other relationship with my master.

But then I see Viola's face, which is overwhelmed in wishes for *everything* about the situation to be different. Hot anger floods through my body, and I lunge over the seats, forgetting to be invisible to Viola.

I grab the collar of Aaron's shirt and yank him off her with more force than necessary, thrusting him back into his seat. Aaron stares at Viola, confused and unable to see me.

"What just happened?" Aaron says, rubbing his head where it rebounded off the red velvet seat.

I could ask you the same thing, I think, breathing hard in anger. But I know what happened, what *really* just happened:

I'm . . . jealous.

Wait. No. I can't be jealous. My fingers tense and I can feel my pulse throbbing under my skin. My heart pounds in my chest and my mind races. The image of Viola and Aaron collides with the realization that I'm *jealous*. Jealousy is a mortal emotion. One that means I feel I have something to lose—something that, if gone, will tear away a part of me. Jealousy is not for my kind. And yet there it is: I'm jealous. Aaron gets to touch her, gets to be seen with her. . . .

I look at Viola, whose eyes are wide in a combination of shock and anger—making it tricky to read any wishes beneath them. She's staring at me with flames in her eyes, but then lets her gaze fall back to Aaron.

"Candy. I want some candy. I'll be right back," she says icily, nearly shaking. Someone in the back of the theater shushes her, but she grits her teeth and looks at me. Fury invades her eyes, casting aside her wishes. She snatches her purse from the adjacent seat, and I follow her as she storms down the lighted stairs to the dark hallway. When we're right beside the exit, she wheels around to face me, her face sharp and shadowed by the light pouring through the door's tiny window.

"What do you think you're doing?" she demands in a harsh whisper.

I wince at the pull of her direct questions—she wants

answers so badly that it hurts me, twisting my stomach around and seizing my muscles. "I'm pulling a guy off you when you clearly don't want to make out while eyeballs are melting right in front of you. You don't want to be here, Viola, I see it—"

"That doesn't matter!" Viola hisses, taking a step closer to me. "It's not your job to pull my boyfriend off me! And you don't get to choose who I make out with! Just because you can read my wishes doesn't mean you get to call the shots!" She leans back against the wall as a teenage stranger with "I wish there was a closer bathroom" written all over his face runs down the dark hall and slams through the exit.

Viola's face whirls back to anger as soon as he's passed. "What makes you think you can chaperone me like that?" she says with an uncharacteristic snarl.

I hesitate. The real answer is: because I'm jealous. But I can't be, I shouldn't be, so instead of saying it, I avoid it.

"You know what? Fine," I snap back at her. "I shouldn't have broken protocol, *master*."

"It has nothing to do with me being your master!" she yells. "You shouldn't have done it because you're my friend!"

"We aren't supposed to *be* friends!" I erupt in frustration. "We aren't supposed to be like this! I'm supposed to grant your wishes and leave, and in two wishes I can do that. I stop breaking protocol, you get your life back, and I get back to Caliban and start acting like a jinn instead of some stupid mortal. It's better for everyone."

"Fine then, I'll wish!" she shouts.

But I disappear before she can.

I HOLD IN a sigh of relief when I realize Jinn is gone. I don't really have a wish, and I'm not sure I would've been able to wish on the spot like that. Anger rushing through me, I storm into the brightly lit theater lobby, which is flooded with the smell of burnt popcorn. I want to go home, right now, but Aaron drove. I yank my cell phone from my purse and call Lawrence—I think Aaron would leave the movie for me, but I hate to make him go before the last teen gets eviscerated.

"Can you come get me?" I say flatly when he answers the phone.

"I thought you were with Aaron," he says in alarm.

"I am, but . . . I've got to get out of here."

"What happened? Did Aaron try anything? Where is Jinn?"

"He's the problem, not Aaron. Look, please, I just want to go home instead of trying to stomach the rest of this awful horror thing we're seeing."

"Be there in fifteen minutes," Lawrence replies nervously, and I hear his car growl to a start. I snap the phone shut and dip back into the theater. Aaron welcomes me by wrapping an arm around my waist and pulling me into him, all without turning away from the movie.

"No," I whisper, trying to resist sinking into his side. "I have to go."

"Huh?" Aaron says, yanking his stare away from the screen. Someone shushes us again.

"It's a . . . family thing, sort of," I mutter, trying to hide the surge of frustration that arises when I think about Jinn spying on me. "I called Lawrence, though. Go ahead and stay."

"Well . . . I should take you home," Aaron says, looking longingly at the screen.

"No, really, it'll be fine."

"Okay," Aaron replies, looking a little relieved. He pulls me forward and kisses me, but I dart back, hyperaware now that Jinn very well could be lingering nearby. How am I supposed to know if he's gone or not? I hurry back to the lobby, trying to avoid the confused glances of the staff as I wait for Lawrence to arrive. When his car pulls up outside, I practically run to it and slide down in the passenger seat, slinging my purse into the back.

I stare straight ahead as Lawrence pulls out of the parking lot, and wait until the silence is thick before I finally vent. "Jinn was there, spying on me. He was invisible."

"Ouch," Lawrence says, but his voice has a strange sense of relief.

Words flood my mouth. "He pulled Aaron off me! Like some sort of big brother or babysitter! I can't believe him!" I growl. I can feel my cheeks turning an even deeper scarlet as I remember seeing Jinn lurking behind us, and then the expression on Aaron's face when he thought *I* shoved him away.

"He was just looking out for you, probably," Lawrence says.

His calm only enrages me more.

"Looking out for me? If I want to make out with my new boyfriend in a theater—"

"Make out? You hate PDA," Lawrence says, raising an eyebrow.

"Whatever, Lawrence. That's not the point. It was a spur-of-the-moment thing. Not that it lasted long, thanks to Jinn. I've finally started feeling . . . I don't know, like I'm in control of my life, but then big brother genie decides to make all my choices for me."

Lawrence turns to me as we roll to a stop at a red light. "Invisible spying, okay, that crosses the line. But I can't exactly hate him for watching out for my best friend. Especially if Aaron was getting you to act like . . . well, to act like someone you aren't."

He says the words like they're supposed to be sweet or endearing. But my jaw clamps shut, and my mind races. Are Lawrence and Jinn in on this together? They both think I need a guy to babysit me on dates, like some sort of 1890s society girl? I fight the tension in my throat.

"It's not Jinn's job to save me—or yours! What, do you think I need a babysitter? That you have to take care of me?" I snap.

Lawrence puts a hand to his forehead. "Not like that—"

"Apparently, *just* like that! I'd rather both of you just leave me alone!"

Lawrence's eyes glitter angrily in a way I rarely see, and I realize I've crossed some sort of line I didn't know existed. "Leave you alone?" Lawrence begins quietly. Something in his voice is more serious, more severe than a response to my anger at him and Jinn for breaking my trust. Some deeper issue is bubbling underneath, ready to rise to the surface. "Do you really want that?" he continues. "I do everything for you, Viola. I drive you around, I listen when you cry, I cancel plans if you're lonely. Without fail, if you need something, I'm *always* there. So now, when you're making out with *Aaron Moor*, acting like someone I don't know, I'm suddenly supposed to leave you alone?" By the time he finishes, he's just short of shouting. Someone behind us lays on the car horn, and Lawrence jerks the car forward when he realizes the light has turned green.

"It doesn't matter!" I snap back as Lawrence takes a sharper turn than normal. "Being my friend and spying on me—"

"Your friend? You don't treat me like a friend, Viola. You've never stopped treating me like your boyfriend!"

My mouth drops open, and I choke on my words as a few tears of anger finally slip down my cheeks. That was low. "I'm so sorry that after *two years together*, it's hard to revert back to friendship, especially when you're trying to control my relationships with other guys!"

"Relationships? Plural? So far Aaron is the only relationship you've had, and you don't even really love him!"

"You *know* that wish was an accident—"

"No, it wasn't! Maybe you didn't really want Aaron specifically, but you've spent the last seven months feeling sorry for yourself, and suddenly here comes this jinn who can fix your problems."

"That's not how it was! I didn't even mean to say it—"

"But you *wanted* it the whole time! You wanted to stop feeling invisible, I get that—but you could've made that happen on your own. Couldn't you have tried to talk to people, tried to move on, tried to be *yourself* instead of almost letting your entire existence end with our relationship? You didn't have to drag Aaron or Ollie or me into this. I mean, did it ever occur to you, Viola, why I suddenly came out, yet you don't see me dating? Haven't you ever wondered?"

"I didn't ask for Aaron—" I protest.

"Because of you!" Lawrence cuts me off, slamming on the brakes at a stop sign in my neighborhood. He shoves the gear shift into park and turns toward me. "Every time I'm interested in a guy, I know that if I tell the one person I *want* to tell about it—my best friend—she'll feel more 'invisible' than before!" A car speeds by, horn blasting at us for stopping in the middle of the street. Lawrence ignores it and continues, quieter this time. "And it's going to happen again, Viola. You don't love Aaron. You'll split with him, and until *you can make yourself happy*, no amount of wishing is going to stop you from feeling invisible in the long run. You've got to let go of the past and stop beating yourself down."

"Let go? I *loved* you, Lawrence, you know that! You *let* me love you—" I argue.

"What was I supposed to do, hold off telling you I'm gay until you fell *out* of love with me—"

"You should have told me sooner!"

"I didn't know—"

"*I* knew!" Tears spring to life in my eyes, and I don't even know what I'm crying about—Jinn spying, Lawrence agreeing with him, or *this*. I continue, "I knew, Lawrence, even if I didn't say it! And if I knew, you knew! You didn't say anything, you let me go on believing—"

"Then you should have gotten out!" Lawrence returns, but his voice has softened. "You had the choice. You just waited for me to make it for you. Just like you waited for wishes to stop being invisible." He looks back to the road, puts the car in drive, and eases forward.

"Don't put this on me," I say through my tears. "I may need you for a lot of things, Lawrence, but you still should have told me. And if it hurts you to see me happy with Aaron, then fine. You hurt me first. You deserve it. *Leave me alone.*"

I look at Lawrence for a long time, but he doesn't turn to me or even appear to take a breath. In just moments, we're pulling into my driveway. Lawrence's jaw flexes, and I realize he's gritting his teeth. He stops the car abruptly but continues to stare through the car windshield, like I'm not even there. I search my mind for something else to say, something to continue the fight, but instead I grab my purse from the backseat and throw the door open. I slam it behind me and watch as Lawrence pulls out of my driveway and speeds off without so much as a glance in my direction.

SIXTEEN

Jinn

"I GOT TOO involved. I don't know why—why do I do this to myself?" I yell to the ifrit in the park. I can't get the scent of Aaron's cheap cologne and the expression in Viola's eyes out of my head, even though it's been hours—the sun has long set into a dark night seeded with stars.

I'm jealous. What's happening to me? Viola is angry at me and I care. I shouldn't care.

"You always had a soft spot for mortals, I think," the ifrit answers, a defeated, disappointed look in his eyes.

"It's what kept me from becoming an ifrit," I mutter. I pace back and forth in front of the oak tree, while the ifrit calmly leans against its trunk, arms folded. There's no fear in Caliban. I wouldn't feel like this in Caliban.

Jealous.

There's definitely no jealousy in Caliban.

"You've got to get home, my friend. You think this is what matters, but getting *home* is what's important, your *kind* are important. Look at me—look how I've aged here! We were once the same age, remember? This isn't what you want, to die as a mortal."

To change. To age. To be different every moment. To be like Viola. The thoughts that had grown to be something beautiful, *desirable*, become ugly and terrifying in the space of a moment. What have I become, that I could have any yearning to age? That I feel broken because of some *girl*? This is not who I am, what I am. I'm a jinn. *A* jinn, not *Jinn*. I have no name, no personal relationships—no matter what I've come to think. How many moments of my life are gone forever because of this?

"Look," the ifrit says. He steps forward and places a hand— the hand of a grown man, not a boy—on my shoulder. "You broke the three protocols about a hundred times—the Ancients are already furious enough about that. You've lost five days of your life. And look at yourself—you're a mess, because you've started caring for a girl who is your master. Your *master*—not your friend. You are always going to be the creature that grants her wishes, no matter what she says or what you want to believe.

"Get home, my friend. Get home to Caliban so you can make sense of your life again. I'll talk to the Ancients, try to get them to go easy on you. I'll tell them you just had a lapse in judgment and are back to following protocol and everything. Just get *home*."

He's right. Of course he's right. He understands; he's a fellow jinn. How could I think a mortal girl could understand what I am? How could I think that in just five days, she and I could be . . . friends?

"Besides, those flowers aren't going to deliver themselves," the ifrit adds with a grin. I force a fake smile through the stampede of thoughts in my head. The ifrit adds, "This is not your world. We aren't mortals, always searching for completion and getting their hearts broken—"

"It's not like that," I snap. "I just . . . I know I'm a wish granter, and she's my master, but at the same time it's like . . . it's like she's my friend." The words are spoken not in affection, but amazement.

She's my friend.

"Well," the ifrit says, looking doubtful at this claim, "what did you think would happen—best case? She'll forget about you when you return to Caliban, you know that. Or do you think she won't wish, that you can stay here with her? That for the rest of her life, she'll put you above getting whatever she wishes for? Even better—that for the rest of her life, she won't slip up and say something like 'I wish it would stop raining'? You can't win this. In the end, you'll be in Caliban. She'll forget you. And whatever 'friendship' you think you have will be gone. Relationships are not for immortals. A bird and a fish may long for each other, but where could they live?"

I gaze across the park. The sun is starting to rise over the pool on the opposite side, and the stars are fading away into a peach-colored morning. Dandelions are growing on the park's sad excuse for a football field. There are no weeds in Caliban either. Caliban, my home. I miss my home. Where things are normal, where I'm not confused, attached to a . . . *mortal*.

I turn back to the ifrit, a solid feeling in my heart and a firm decision in my mind. "Do it. Press her."

"A wise decision, my—"

"But don't hurt her," I interrupt, as my mind jumps to the thought of the ifrit pressing Viola by way of some grisly accident. "I know it shouldn't matter, but please. Don't hurt her."

The ifrit raises an eyebrow and looks annoyed, but then nods. "All right. Give me a few days, I'll come up with something that won't hurt her." The ifrit studies me for a moment more, then vanishes.

I collapse onto the ground and stare at the starless morning sky. Soon. Soon, I can go home again. It feels as if someone has pushed a boulder off my chest that was weighing me down to the mortal world. It's easier this way. It's easier to be jinn than mortal. I'm happier this way.

SEVENTEEN
Viola

I CAN'T SLEEP. It's late now, and even though my body aches and it begs me to rest, my mind continues to storm with thoughts of Lawrence and Jinn. I can't stop tears from filling my eyes every few minutes. I keep looking to the armchair Jinn usually sits in, how he sat there the night before while I slept, because . . . because I trusted him. Because I forgot what he was. Because I never thought he'd use his powers against me, to trick me. He was just *Jinn*, my friend, not some magical invisible creature. But not anymore. And Lawrence, too . . . something that feels like guilt and anger has settled deep in my stomach, weighing me down until I feel sick and clammy. I curl my knees into my chest and force my eyes shut.

It's hard to sleep—I keep jolting awake, both dreading and hoping to see Jinn in my bedroom. Morning comes far too quickly, and Aaron pulls into my driveway before I've even combed my hair. It's raining outside, a misty, light rain that turns the sky the same color as the asphalt and makes my skin feel sticky.

"Are you sure you're okay?" Aaron asks when I toss my bag into his car. I'm not sure if he's asking because my eyes are still puffy and red despite a layer of makeup, or if he's referring to me ditching him yesterday.

"Oh, yeah. Everything is fine," I say, with a sinking feeling in my stomach, and try to give a lighthearted shrug. Aaron grins, nods, and reverses the car out of the driveway so quickly that my stomach spins until I'm so nauseous I beg him to slow down.

"Sorry," Aaron says, and drops the speed down by a few miles per hour. "Do you want me to tell you about the end of the movie? I was worried after you left." He reaches over and rubs my forearm affectionately.

"No, I'm good," I say, sharper than I intended. I try to edge my arm away—for all I know, Jinn is in the backseat. Though I'm not sure why it matters; if he wants to spy on me and Aaron, he deserves to see us acting like a couple is supposed to act. I exhale as anger and hurt fill me again, and wrap Aaron's hand tightly in my own. When we park in the student lot, Aaron leans over to kiss me, and after a moment's pause I let him, some hateful part of me hoping Jinn is watching. But no one shoves Aaron; no invisible hand knocks him away. We just kiss, and after we get out of the car I can't help but feel disappointed. It's hard to be vengeful when Jinn actually *is* staying away from me.

I fake my way through Wednesday with the Royal Family— when they ask me what's wrong, I just claim I have allergies or a bad cold. It shuts them up, though a few explain how they just skip school if they're so sick that people can tell. Somehow this is not as comforting as they seem to think it'll be.

I'm not surprised that Lawrence avoids me; after all, according to him I'm responsible for his lack of a dating life. At lunch, he sits at the opposite end of the table, leaving me surrounded with Aaron and cookie-cutter blonde girls. He picks at his food and leaves early, all without glancing my way. One of the blondes notices and suggests I go talk to him. "I mean, you two are, like, really close, aren't you?" she says, rolling a carrot stick between her fingers.

I shrug and try to act casual. "Not so much anymore." The girl shrugs and goes back to eating her lunch of raw vegetables (a diet she swears by), and I watch Lawrence disappear down the hallway. I'm still angry at him—fuming, even—for the way he made me feel, for thinking I need to be babysat, for not telling me when he knew he couldn't love me. But for some reason, my stomach twinges in guilt. I quickly ask how the veggie diet is going so I don't feel compelled to follow him.

Thursday is much the same. When I wake up, I scan the room for Jinn, but the house is empty; knowing this causes a sort of hollow feeling to creep up on me as I get ready for school. I silently mouth Jinn's name in my Shakespeare class, where I first saw him, letting just enough of a breathy whisper escape my lips so that if he appears I can pretend it was an accident. Somehow the fact that he doesn't appear makes me even angrier—what right does he have to hold a grudge against me? He's the one who was out of line. I even let Aaron kiss me in the school hallways to the point that people begin to whistle, figuring that Lawrence or Jinn will want to put a stop to it more than they want to continue the silent treatment. But no luck there, either.

"I'll see you tomorrow night, baby," Aaron says as I get out of his Jeep on Friday afternoon. The rain has mostly let up, but the world is still gray and soggy. Aaron puts the Jeep in park and comes around to the passenger side to press me against the car and kiss me hard. I turn away before it goes on too long.

"Yeah, see you there," I reply reluctantly. We have plans to go to some party. Amazing how I went from longing for an invitation to wishing I could avoid a party, all in the same week.

"Awesome. Need me to pick you up?"

"Um . . . yeah. Yeah."

"Awesome," he says again. "I'll come get you at nine."

"Okay. I'll see you later."

"Awesome."

Great word, Aaron. I dodge a last kiss and go inside, dropping my bag in the kitchen and collapsing on the couch to watch TV . . . alone. And lonely.

I could say his name and he'll have to come. Not that I really want him to show up simply because I gave him an order, but . . . he'd still have to come. I sigh and bury my face in a couch pillow as the sinking realization washes over me for the thousandth time today: Without Lawrence and Jinn, I feel sick and alone, so much so that it covers up any anger I might have. They own a space in me that Aaron and my new Royal Family friends can't fill with lip gloss or beer, a space that's raw and aching. Like I'm being broken all over again.

Saturday morning arrives too soon. When I wake up, my eyes instantly go to the armchair. Still empty. I sigh and force myself to look away, catching sight of a few old painting projects piled up in the corner of my bedroom.

I haven't painted in days, I realize. Suddenly I miss the feeling of painting more than I knew until this moment, and the urge to grab for a brush sweeps over me like the need to eat or drink. But all of my paints are at school.

I could go to the school; there are enough weekend activities that a door is always unlocked. Paint all evening. Skip the party tonight. Of course, it's not what the new shiny Viola should do. But it would give me something to do all day rather than bite my lip over the fact that I can't talk to Jinn or Lawrence.

Yes. I'm going. I grab my mother's car keys without asking, and a half hour later I slip into the school. My Expo paintings sit patiently, covered with ripped-up bedsheets. I yank the sheets off.

I don't like these. They're just paintings. Pretty enough, but just paintings. They aren't expressions or emotions . . . or me. I mean, they told us to paint landscapes, and I obeyed; I painted landscapes. Landscapes that belong on walls in living rooms, or above bedroom dressers. They don't belong to me. They aren't paintings that show the world who I am, what I am. I grab all five canvases from their easels, dropping them in a stack on a nearby table, and fill the easels with fresh, blank canvases— clean slates ready to be filled up.

The Expo is in just a few days. I'm not talented enough to come up with something amazing in that amount of time. I've got no business starting from scratch this late. But the desire to fill the blank canvas with color tingles through my chest, down my arms, until it feels like it may explode from my fingertips. I reach for a brush and splash color across the whiteness.

Hours pass, though I hardly notice. My hands are speckled in colors that match the bright sunset outside. The paintings are strange; something to do with me, Ollie, Lawrence, Aaron . . . something to do with Jinn. Something to do with studying pink hair and chain belts and French manicures, and how everything is a marker to show who you are, what you belong to. The emotions spill out onto the white until they don't consume my head anymore, until I don't care if the paintings are good or not.

My cell phone rings, and my brush clatters to the concrete floor.

"Hello?" I answer, rubbing my face, probably getting paint all over it.

"Hey, beautiful," Aaron's voice says.

Viola. My name is Viola.

"Still want me to pick you up?"

I look longingly at the painting; it's not quite finished. "Actually . . . I'm working on a painting. I can't go," I say.

Aaron sighs deeply. "But, baby, I just want to be with you tonight, you know? I love you."

"Yeah." But only because I wished for it.

"Can't you work on the painting another day?"

I can. I can do that. But I don't want to; I want to paint now, while all the emotion is stirred up. Jinn would understand that. So would Lawrence. But I can leave. I sigh as guilt fills me. It's my fault that he loves me, that he wants me there. It's not his fault for not understanding me, or why I paint. I owe it to him.

"Yes," I reply, holding in a heavy sigh. "I'll meet you at my house."

I try to look excited as I climb out of Aaron's Jeep a half hour later. Boys rush to help Aaron with a cooler, and girls shout for me to join their tiny circle of pretty people. But I can stand the gossip for only so long before I migrate away from them, grateful to see that the backyard is almost empty, save for a few couples making out and a lone girl in a tiny flower garden.

It's a dark, cloudless night, and the moon is only a tiny sliver in the sky. The house is set far enough out that the nearest streetlights are just specks in the distance, and with so few of the house's lights on, the stars look especially brilliant. I sigh, gazing at them, then hear a sob from the girl in the flower garden. I raise my eyebrows and take several steps toward the girl while the nearest makeout pair moves away from her.

"Hello?" I call out. The girl doesn't answer, just gives another small sob. I step closer, through the garden's soft soil. The headlights of an arriving car shine across the girl's tearstained face. Her skin is dull and her eyes are empty, but she reminds me of someone. . . .

I throw a hand to my mouth.

I think it's Ollie—no, I *know* it's Ollie—but this isn't . . . this isn't her. This isn't the girl I know, disheveled and weeping in the grass. Her skin is dull, her eyes look as though they're aching, and she chokes on a sob before laying her head to the ground in what looks like defeat.

My wish wasn't supposed to hurt anybody. I sink to my knees beside the girl, who hardly seems to notice I'm here.

It's my fault. It's all my fault.

Jinn. Jinn, help. Please.

EIGHTEEN

Jinn

A ROLL OF thunder rattles through the park, startling the ducks that I was trying to coax toward me. I look up expectantly, but no raindrops fall. I sigh and sit back in the cool grass to wait. Again. For the fourth day in a row.

This is normal, no matter how boring it is, I remind myself. This is how it should be while I wait for my master to wish—sitting alone. It's good that I asked for the press. I've been repeating that to myself all day, because I know that if I let the lingering doubt in my head speak up, I'll crumble. It's easier to stay bitter—to think of Viola yelling at me, of the days I've lost, of Caliban. To ignore the fact that two people know me—that two people, until Tuesday, considered me their friend. I suppose one of the two still does.

Lawrence. I showed myself to him. I involved him, and now he might be used to press Viola. She'd wish to help him, to save him. Another bolt of jealousy rushes through me. Viola and Lawrence would wish to save each other. Would they do the same for me? Would anyone?

That's for mortals. See what being here has done to you?

But I still should warn Lawrence, as I remember the time he called me "friend." Plus, I'm incredibly bored and I haven't had a conversation with anyone in days. I'm already in so much trouble with the Ancients when I get back, what's one more offense? I vanish from the park. Lawrence yells and trips over a baseball bat when I appear in his bedroom.

"You could warn me," he mutters, rubbing his knee where it crashed into the carpet.

"Sorry, I forgot," I answer, trying to hide how much of a relief it is for someone to see me again. Lawrence rolls his eyes and pulls himself up into his computer chair.

"It's good to see you, though, really. As long as . . . don't tell me she's made another wish?" he asks.

I shake my head. "No . . . no. That's not why I'm here. We haven't . . . I mean, she hasn't called for me in days."

"Me either. She usually can't hold a grudge, but I'm starting to wonder. She's going to a party tonight, so I'm not going since . . . it's awkward. But if you want to watch *Family Guy* reruns with me, you're more than welcome."

The offer is tempting, but I hesitate. "Actually, that's not why I'm here." How do I explain that I might have requested to have him hurt? "Viola is going to wish soon," I say slowly.

Lawrence raises an eyebrow. "Oh?"

"It's for the better, I mean. Two more wishes and I go back home. And besides, she has Aaron now; she doesn't need a jinn following her around."

Lawrence laughs and sits back down on the edge of his bed. "Yeah, she may say she loves Aaron, but she looks at you the way she used to look at me," Lawrence says with a sad sort of smile. "You know, before I became a raging homosexual." Lawrence grins, but I can't even smile back because my head is suddenly too full.

She looks at me the way she used to look at him. The person she loved.

No one has ever looked at me that way. Something inside me pulses, and I turn away from Lawrence as a warm feeling rushes from my head to my fingertips.

No. No. Relationships are for mortals.

I turn back to Lawrence and shake my head. "A bird and a fish might love each other, but where could they live?"

"I don't know, an underwater birdcage?" Lawrence replies.

I sigh and put my head in my hand.

Lawrence stands, folding his arms. "Jinn, is something wrong—"

"I asked for a press," I say as fast as I can. *Don't look at Lawrence.*

"You asked for a what?"

I focus on the old baseball trophies behind Lawrence's head. "Whenever there's a concern about a master not wishing, the ifrit get involved. They press a person to wish—put the person in a situation that he or she will need to wish some way out of. It's not always that pretty, but the ifrit really are trying to do good. It's their job, helping earthbound jinn escape. I asked them to press Viola."

"You asked them to hurt—" Lawrence's voice raises, his eyes wide and panicky.

"No!" I snap. Who does Lawrence think I am? "I got the ifrit's word that he wouldn't press Viola directly, that he won't hurt her. It's for the best, Lawrence. There are rules in Caliban, protocol that the Ancients enforce and we have to follow while earthbound. This isn't my world—"

"But she's your friend! You have to warn her! What's wrong with you?" Lawrence shouts, stepping closer to me with each word.

I open my mouth to speak again, but freeze.

Viola.

Her call rips through my head like a scream that causes my mouth to dry and my palms to sweat. A press. It must be a press. My stomach lurches. *It's for the better, remember?* He promised not to hurt her. *It's for the better,* I chant to myself, but the sick feeling intensifies. How could I? What have I done? She's my friend.

The words leave my mouth in a whisper. "She's calling for me."

"She's at Aaron's party. I'll meet you there," Lawrence says, grabbing his car keys off his desk. I nod as the world blurs and I vanish.

I expect to arrive in the center of a party like the one before Viola's first wish—red cups everywhere, music thumping, Aaron draped with girls like they're human ivy. Instead, I appear in a starlit garden. Music from the house in front of it thumps dully through the walls, and there's a hum of conversation that's almost hidden by the chirps of crickets. Viola is kneeling by a bed of tulips and hydrangeas, her head turned away. She doesn't even realize I'm behind her. Before I can speak, a voice cuts me off.

"I tried to talk to him, he told me to fuck off. What did I do? I don't understand. We were supposed to be forever," the voice weeps from between rows of canna lilies. The speaker is . . . *no*.

It's Ollie. But not the beautiful, mysterious, and bright Ollie that I remember from last week.

This Ollie has mascara streaming down her cheeks. Her eyes are glassy and red from crying, and her face is ugly with grief. Her clothes look different on her—she looks like a lost little girl in her mother's hand-me-downs. A thunderhead rolls in front of the moon and throws Ollie's and Viola's faces into shadow.

"Master," I say, choking out the title instead of her name.

Remember, it's easier when she's just your master, when she's not "Viola." Protocol. Viola turns to me, her face twisted in misery. I want to call her name, so, so badly. And I want her to say mine. I breathe in.

"*Viola.* Please," she begs, and her voice is trembling. Suddenly nothing else matters—the ifrit, Caliban, aging. How could I have thought any of that truly mattered? I don't know what to do—reach toward her? Stand quietly? Keep speaking, stay silent? What can I do to stop her pain?

Suddenly my body knows what to do even though my head doesn't. I drop to my knees beside her and put a hand on top of hers as the clouds start to drip. Movement from behind the rosebushes catches my eye—it's the ifrit. His silk tunic reflects

175

the lights from the house, and he folds his arms, giving me a long, perplexed gaze. I leave my hand firmly on Viola's and look away from him.

"It's my fault she's like this. I ruined Ollie. Look at her," Viola murmurs as Ollie buries her head in her hands. The white artist's palette tattoo on her back looks faded and sickly. A clap of thunder bangs in the distance. People who were partying outside rush into the house, and the music gets louder.

"I don't understand," Ollie weeps. "I feel so . . . so . . ."

"Broken," Viola whispers. She sits back and puts her head in her hands. "What have I done?"

I respond grimly, "You made a wish."

And I asked for a press.

"But I never wanted to hurt Ollie. I never wanted to hurt anyone. I just wanted to feel whole again. But I don't, even though I belong now." The rain begins to transform from a light sprinkle to a hard summer rain. There's no rain in Caliban, either. Water falls on Viola's eyelashes, mixing in with her tears.

"Can I take it back? Wish to undo the first wish?" Viola asks.

"No. No, you can't," I breathe. "You can't unwish something."

Viola's gaze falls to Ollie again.

"I have to make it right," she says fearfully. "What do I have to do?" she asks, looking back at me.

Viola doesn't really want to know—her question hardly pulls at me. Probably because she already knows what she has to do. She just needs to hear it, to know there's no other way.

"You'd have to wish again," I say, then look away. A feeling I don't know grips me as the words leave my mouth, some sort of writhing between my stomach and my heart. The ifrit gives me a stern look and vanishes. Viola inhales deeply and doesn't speak for several moments.

"I'm sorry," she finally says firmly. Can she read me the way I read her? Does she know how badly I don't want her to wish? Her voice drops to a whisper. "I have to."

"I understand," I answer. He's a great ifrit. It was a good press. And it's my own fault that she wished, that I'm losing her for a world of stillness and solidarity. I stand. I don't want to do this. I want to be anything but a wish granter at this moment.

Viola doesn't look at me, but rather at Ollie, whose hands and clothes are muddy and whose face is swollen from tears. She reaches out and puts a hand on Ollie's arm.

"I wish for Ollie to be okay," she says breathily, closing her eyes as she does so. She doesn't look at me—I'm glad, because I know my face is contorted into a horrible grimace. I fight it, even though I know there's no point—the wish pulls at me like a strong wave. I wait until the last moment to grant it, until the wave feeling rushes over me so strongly that I feel I might drown. Finally, I wrap one arm over my stomach, the other against my back and bow slowly.

To Viola. To my *master*. How could I hurt her? What have I done?

"As you wish."

NINETEEN
Viola

I LOOK INTO Jinn's eyes as the words leave his mouth. He looks at me differently than Aaron does. As if I could have any hair color, be any size, be sick or healthy, be fat, skinny, or dying, and he would still look at me the same way. The rain makes his golden skin seem slick and polished, and he looks less human than he ever has before. He rises from the bow and breaks eye contact with me to stare into the sky.

"It doesn't rain in Caliban," he says, letting raindrops splash onto his face. I follow his gaze to the clouds, then remember Ollie. My eyes dart to the bushes where Ollie was, dirty and weeping. She's gone. A bright, apple-colored laugh resounds through the garden from somewhere in the house. I look inside.

Ollie is sitting on the kitchen counter, framed by the window's pink curtains. Her hair falls in perfectly tousled curls, and her teeth are shiny and white. Her skin is back to its honey color, and when she turns around, I see the white tattoo on her back, as shimmery as ever. Boys surround her, and she smiles at them, then hops off the counter and vanishes from my line of sight.

"It worked," I say softly. Jinn looks away from the sky, droplets of rain rolling down his cheeks, like tears.

"Yes." He inhales and talks quickly, in a voice too casual to be genuinely so. "I covered up the memory of Aaron leaving her. I can't erase memories, not really. . . . Jinn magic isn't that strong—"

"I'm sorry," I interrupt him, voice breathless.

"Don't be," Jinn answers, staring at the wet grass. "It's my fault." His jaw is tight, and there's a hurt look in his eyes. I watch him carefully through the increasing rain, longing to read his desires as he reads mine.

"What do you mean?" I ask, searching his face. *It's not your fault. It's my fault.*

Jinn pauses and rubs his face with his hand. "Viola . . . Ollie was a press. I asked another jinn to get you to wish. I was confused. I was jealous. I didn't understand. I thought I had to get home; I thought I needed you to wish."

My breath quavers in my throat as water runs off my hair and down my back. He did *what* to me?

"I don't understand," I whisper.

Jinn bites his lip, then launches into an explanation: ifrit, pressing, time, wishes, Caliban. The words run together like the scent of liquor and smoke from the house. *He wanted to leave. He wanted me to wish so he could leave.* The knowledge twists into me like a knife; he said he liked being here. I thought he liked being with me. I thought he didn't want to leave anymore. I force myself to swallow.

"I asked him not to hurt *you*, so he made *Ollie* hurt over the breakup with Aaron, just to get to you. It's my fault. I'm so sorry, Viola," Jinn says loudly, to be heard over the sound of the rainstorm.

Jinn did this. And he did it intentionally. I can't find my voice, and I can barely see; everything is blurred and obscured by the raindrops. Everything but Jinn. He's breathing deeply and gazing into my eyes as he speaks. His voice is rough and low, and his fingers twitch as if he's longing to reach toward me. I take a step away from him and fold my arms over my waist. A clap of thunder erupts overhead.

I finally find words. "I would have . . . you want to go. You wanted me to hurt so you could . . . ," I trail off as a flash of lightning illuminates the garden. I shiver, though I'm not certain it's from the cold.

"No, Viola, please. It was a mistake. I was scared because . . ." He looks down. "Because I'm beginning to feel like I'm broken without you. Like something about me, about who and what I am, is going to be gone if I leave you. With you, I'm not just a wish granter. And I'm not supposed to feel that. A wish granter is what I am. I'm *not* a mortal, but I . . . it's almost like I *wish* I was one." He says the words with a look of confusion on his face, and I can't help wondering if he's ever had a wish before.

My name shoots across the yard in a slurred voice. Aaron is standing at the door, beer in hand. I groan.

"Viola! You coming back in?" he shouts. I turn to Jinn.

You betrayed me.

"Viola?" Aaron's voice calls again. "You all right?"

"I'm fine!" I lie, glancing back at Aaron. When I look back to Jinn, he's gone.

I exhale and shake the tears from my eyes, then turn and walk toward Aaron.

"Why didn't you come in when it started raining, baby? You're soaked." Aaron asks as he holds open the screen door. He rubs his hands on my shoulders to warm them.

"I got distracted," I mumble. Aaron calls out to one of his Aaron Moor Boys, who retrieves a towel. Aaron runs the towel through my hair—tangling it—and then wraps it around me, though I feel so numb I barely notice. He leads me out of the kitchen, and we collapse together on the couch. From somewhere behind me, I hear two girls talking and pick up the phrase "Aaron Moor's Girlfriend."

Exactly, I think. This is a party for Aaron Moor's Girlfriend.

For shiny Viola. I thought that was me, but . . . it's not. I'm not really shiny Viola, and I'm not the old Viola, either. I'm not even an Invisible Girl anymore. I'm just—

"Viola?" A voice calls my name. I look up.

It's Lawrence, eyes full of concern, a frantic look on his face. He extends a hand to me, and without hesitation I take it and stand.

"You going somewhere?" Aaron asks as he swigs his beer.

"Home. Sick," I lie. I don't care.

"Aw, you want me to drive you? I can take care of you," he says as he swigs the beer again. I shake my head.

"Where is Jinn?" Lawrence asks as we walk out the front door.

"I don't know. He was here, but then after I made the wish for Ollie, he vanished." We climb in the car and, seeing I'm shivering, Lawrence turns the heat on high.

"So you wished?" Lawrence says after a few moments of silence.

"Yes," I answer softly. "I had to. Ollie was . . . she was a

184

disaster because of losing Aaron. It was horrible. And it was Jinn's doing."

"A press. Jinn told me."

"He betrayed me. He hurt me."

"Viola . . . I . . . I don't think he meant it. When you called for him . . . you should have seen his eyes."

"But he still hurt me."

"He was scared. He cares for you so much that it scared him. Because you're the first, I think. The only."

I wrap my hair around my fingers. How could someone feel that strongly about me? And how could I feel that way about someone who tried to hurt me?

Because Jinn understands me, in a way that Aaron never will understand me. He knows what I want, what I need, when I need help, when I want to be left alone. I sigh. How could I not care about someone who knows me like that? Someone who cares just as much about me, so much so that I could break him?

It's silent for the rest of the ride, until we pull into my

driveway. I look down and brush my hair behind my ears. I owe Lawrence. For the ride home, but also for so much more.

"Thank you," I say quietly.

"I couldn't let Aaron drive you home," Lawrence says.

"Well . . . yeah, that. But also, just . . . thanks," I answer. Lawrence doesn't reply. I open my door and swing my feet out of the car.

"Vi!" Lawrence calls out just as I'm about to shut the car door. Lawrence looks me in the eye for a long moment. "I'm sorry, Vi."

I nod and smile a little, then shut the door. Lawrence grins and waves good-bye as he pulls out of the driveway.

I slip past my parents, who have fallen asleep with CNN on the TV. I change into fuzzy pajamas in the bathroom, the kind with frogs wearing crowns on them, the kind that I'd never want Aaron to see me in. I sit on the edge of my bed, and my eyes move to the armchair Jinn usually sits in.

I close my eyes and call his name.

TWENTY
Jinn

WHEN I VANISH from the flower garden, the music and the scent of alcohol are replaced with the cool silence of Holly Park. One swing is swaying back and forth slightly. In a blink, the ifrit comes into view sitting on the swing. His bronze eyes flicker up to me like firelight, and he stands. I'm angry, so angry that I can feel the emotion coursing through me, like my blood has turned to poison.

"You requested it, my friend."

"I take the request back. Leave her alone," I growl.

"Hey." The ifrit raises his eyebrows in surprise. "Come on now. You wanted this—"

"Stay away from her!" I shout. My voice echoes across the empty park.

I requested it. I requested the press. But that doesn't mean I can't fight for her now.

The ifrit rises from the swing slowly. I'm tall, but the ifrit is slightly taller—after all, he's a full-grown adult now. We stare hard at each other.

"You're acting human," the ifrit says testily.

"I don't care," I hiss. "Stay away from her."

"Why? Because you think she's keeping you around as her friend? You're her slave. And eventually, she'll wish, and you'll be sent back to Caliban with months, maybe even years taken off your life—and nothing to show for it but a collection of nights spent in a park because she throws you out of her house when she's got no need for you."

I don't care anymore. It's worth it. Even if she never speaks to me again because of the press, she's worth it. She makes me a *person*, not just a wish granter. I never realized how unfulfilling life as a wish granter was until I had something more. Till I had the piece I didn't know I was missing.

"It doesn't matter," I snap. "I shouldn't have asked you to press her. With her, it's not like most mortals. She's not like that."

"They're *all* like that. Greedy, aging, desperate, selfish. It's what they are, just as we are what we are."

My mind clouds over, and I'm shaking with something like frustration or rage or pain. Wood chips grind beneath my knees. My hand makes contact with skin, and pain ricochets through my arm. The next thing I'm aware of is the ifrit, pinned to the ground beneath me.

I hit him. I hit a fellow jinn.

I freeze, stunned as I comprehend what I've just done. I hardly even feel it when the ifrit pushes me off. The ifrit scrambles to stand, eyes wide. He touches his lower lip tenderly, and inhales in shock when he realizes he's bleeding.

No one bleeds in Caliban.

"You hit me," the ifrit murmurs. I grimace and haul myself up from the dirt.

"I can't believe you hit me," the ifrit says, eyes widening even farther. Finally his surprise dissipates to anger. "What's wrong with you?"

"She's not like that," I grumble aloud, running a hand through my hair nervously. I hit an ifrit. I've never even heard of someone hitting an ifrit. But he deserved it. I deserve it, really. I was the one who asked for the press.

"You hit a fellow jinn? Over a human girl? What has this girl done to you?" the ifrit says, finally wiping the blood from his mouth with the hem of his tunic. "You're coming back to Caliban. One way or another, I won't let a human ruin you like this. First you break all three protocols, now this. Do you realize how much trouble you're already in with the Ancients? The mortal girl doesn't matter!"

I breathe in sharply. The mortal girl doesn't matter? No, my friend. She does matter.

"Please," I say aloud. I raise my eyes and meet the ifrit's gaze. "Please don't hurt her. Stop the press. I'll deal with the Ancients when I get back; I'll leave you out of it. But stop the press."

The ifrit looks astounded that I would make a request after punching him—I can't blame him. He shakes his head, like he's staring at a stranger, someone he thinks he might have known in the past. It's a long time before he speaks.

"You can't take back a request for a press. You know that. The Ancients would never allow it, and I can't hide that sort of thing from them. And I wouldn't take it back even if it was possible. You need to get out of here. You think you're happy, right? You're not. You're just confused. Get her to wish, get her to forget you—for your own sake," the ifrit finishes. He wipes his lip again and disappears.

I gasp when he vanishes, like I'm surfacing for air, and lean back against the oak tree. My fingertips tremble slightly. He's right. Of course he's right. She's going to forget me. The connection between a master and a jinn has to be severed at some point. Nothing changes that. It's like I'm being punished.

No—I *am* being punished.

This is why Caliban was a punishment. I realize it now—it's a beautiful, perfect world of nothingness. No connection, no longing, no . . . love. A world we're trapped in until we're needed here, a world we're condemned to while everyone we might care about forgets us. I stare at the stars again. *Please let her forgive me for all this before she forgets me.*

Please.

She calls for me.

I vanish and reappear in her bedroom.

"You left," she says. I nod. Viola's hair is wet, her eyes tired. She looks prettier now than she does when she's trying not to be invisible.

"You hurt me."

I nod again and press my lips together. I think, *Yell.* Somehow, it'd be easier if she just yelled. I drop into the armchair, head in my hands.

"I think we're always looking for new pieces," Viola says quietly.

What?

She continues, "I was looking for Lawrence, then for something to replace Lawrence, then for Aaron . . . maybe that's the real truth about being broken. We're always whole, we're just looking to add on to ourselves, to be *more* whole. And then when a piece leaves, it's broken away. But we aren't left any less whole than we were to begin with. . . ."

"But feeling broken—" I begin, the words tight in my throat. I'm grateful that Viola cuts me off.

"Is horrible. Painful," she finishes. "But then, when you aren't expecting it, new pieces appear and suddenly . . . they're attached." Her eyes rise to meet mine. "And you end up more whole than you were before." She moves closer to the chair I'm sitting in. "You knew me all along—knew Viola, not some crazy incarnation of myself as the old me or the shiny new me or the invisible me. You saw the part of me that was already whole." Viola looks away and smiles—sadly—but she smiles.

I'm forgiven. Relief rushes through me like warm water. Somehow, I'm forgiven.

"Can you ask the ifrit to stop?" Viola asks, her voice soft.

"No. And even if I could, he wouldn't. He's just doing his job. Trying to save me. He'll keep pressing until you make a third wish and I go back."

"If I wish, then I forget you," she murmurs.

"I know," I answer.

But I won't forget you. Jinn don't forget.

Viola is silent. I feel like I should say something, but what could be said?

"You're bleeding."

"What?"

"You're bleeding," Viola repeats, and points at my arm. My shirt is torn and my skin is scratched from the scuffle with the ifrit.

"Oh. I'm fine. I . . . I got in a fight with the ifrit that pressed you," I explain, blushing despite myself.

"Did you win?" she asks.

"Honestly, I think the winner was the pile of wood chips we fell into."

Viola laughs—what a relief, to hear her laugh—and stands up. She sorts through a dresser drawer for a moment before pulling out a different shirt.

"It's Lawrence's. You can wear it if you want."

I nod and stand, and we meet in the center of the bedroom. She brushes her hair back as she hands me the shirt, but when I lay my hand on it, she doesn't let go. Neither of us moves or breathes; it's as if we're frozen by the black fabric between us. My thoughts blur together.

"Sorry," Viola says briskly, and pulls away from the fabric, her cheeks turning carnation pink. I exhale and try to avoid her eyes as she sits back down.

"I'll go clean this up," I say, motioning toward my arm. I step into the bathroom, closing the door behind me and leaning against it for a moment.

She's mortal. But I don't care.

I turn on the water and haphazardly splash it onto my arm, pausing to admire the bleeding. By the time I emerge in Lawrence's clothing, Viola has cut the lights off and is in bed, though I can tell she's still awake. I sit down in the armchair and look at the stars, visible through the split in her curtains.

"You're supposed to be able to wish on stars, you know," Viola says.

"Does it work?" I ask, turning to face her.

"Not really. But we do it anyway," she answers. "There's nothing like that in Caliban?"

"Not really. There are no stars in Caliban. We're not

supposed to tell you about our world, you know," I grin and look up at the stars again. "We're not supposed to do any of this. Whatever this is. I'm not supposed to think of you as anything but a master."

I shouldn't have said it. I shouldn't have said it. Why did I say it? The words slipped out like they were nothing, but the confession causes both me and Viola to look down. A strange feeling swoops around my heart and makes me both dizzy and scared.

"And what do you think of me as?" Viola asks delicately.

Tell her. But do I even know how? I don't think I have the words to use.

"I . . . you're . . . my friend," I say.

Moron.

"Oh," she says, and her voice is rimmed in disappointment. Viola brushes her hair from her face and draws her knees to her chest. She inhales deeply. "Stay."

My head snaps up at the word. She's changed, aged, and the beauty of it makes me smile.

"I'll wait till you fall asleep," I say.

"No. Stay with me," she says, and suddenly I realize she doesn't mean for the night. I rub my forehead so she doesn't see, burning in my eyes, the longing I feel.

"It's not possible. It's not what I am," I say hoarsely. "The no-mermaid rule, remember?"

The streetlamp outside flickers and dies. We're cast into darkness with only faint blue moonlight silhouetting Viola, who is still clutching her knees in a very little-girlish way.

"What else will he do to press me?"

"Anything. He can't hurt *you* directly, because he gave me his word. But he'll probably get to you through Lawrence, since he knows you care about him."

Viola sighs. "I don't even care about the wish," she says in a shaky voice. "All the wishes to be whole that I thought I needed, I don't. Not now. I just don't want you to go."

Perhaps it's because it's dark and it's easier when you don't have to see someone's face, or perhaps it's because I finally snap when her voice sounds tiny and sad, but I sweep from my chair to the bed in one motion. I put a hand on Viola's forearm tentatively—what am I supposed to do? I want to make it right.

Viola unfolds and falls toward me. I'm so startled I almost sit motionless, mannequin-like, but at the last moment I react. I wrap my arms into her fall and hold her close to my chest, until I can feel her heart beating against me. We sit in silence.

What are you doing? I ask myself, but the question is overwhelmed by another inner voice that doesn't speak so much as pulse a feeling of rightness. I've held female jinn close, yes, but I've never had this feeling of not being able to hold someone close enough. I drop my head to the back of her neck and inhale the scent of her skin.

She's a human.

I don't care.

Viola is silent, her head buried against my chest as she breathes deeply. Her hair smells like coconut, and I can feel the calluses on her hands from holding a paintbrush. I can even feel her changing, and I pull her closer to make the feeling stronger.

Moments pass. Neither of us says anything because there seems to be nothing to say. Viola's breathing changes, slows, quiets, and she drifts to sleep. I don't want to move, afraid I'll wake her and she'll pull away, so I hold her for a moment longer. I wonder if this is what sleep on Earth always feels like—soft and delicate, like baby's breath flowers. It looks so different from how sleep feels in Caliban. It's almost four in the morning by the time I finally move her from me, laying her head back on her pillow and sweeping a quilt over her.

I rise, thinking I'll go sit in the armchair until she wakes . . . but no. Instead, I lie down beside her. I can't sleep on Earth, I know, but it doesn't really matter. I stare at the ceiling and listen to her breathe until the sun rises.

TWENTY-ONE
Viola

WHEN I WAKE up, my skin tingles where Jinn's arms were wrapped around me, like someone is drawing tiny spirals on my skin. Wait . . . that didn't happen.

No, that did happen. Jinn held me like . . . I can't think of a word that fits, but a warm, comfortable feeling swells up inside me, and I feel even more whole than I did last night, in his arms. I finally open my eyes and realize Jinn is lying beside me, facing the opposite wall so I can only see thick, curly black hair that looks as soft as spun silk. I'm afraid to speak or move, scared that if I wake him he'll shy away, and I'll blush, and we'll talk about how what happened last night should never happen again.

"I can feel it when you wake up, you know." Jinn's voice surprises me. I feel my face turn red, and I sigh. My hands itch with the desire to touch him again, for him to touch me, but neither of us moves. We lay, me beneath the blankets, him on top of them, connected by fibers of fabric that ricochet energy between us.

Just touch *him*.

My cell phone rings. The energy is ripped apart like torn paper as I kick the blankets off and dart across the room, stumbling when I realize my left foot is asleep. Jinn stands, running a hand through his hair and then collapsing into the armchair as I answer.

"Hey, baby," a voice says. It's Aaron. He sounds tired and not totally sobered up yet.

"Hi," I answer, turning my back toward Jinn and dropping my voice.

"You left early last night. You missed it—Audrey got wasted, it was hilarious." I can tell by the tone of his voice that he's doing that cocky grin thing.

"Yeah . . . sorry."

"We're still on for a movie or whatever this afternoon, right?"

I stop. I turn and look hesitantly at Jinn. The dark pools of his eyes flicker up at me.

"I can't," I say. Jinn's eyes soften and he smiles at me. "I can't. I have plans."

"Come on. . . . " His voice is sly and smooth, like he's coaxing a wild animal.

"I have to go—I'll call you later," I say, and before he can speak again, I flip my phone shut.

"After wishing for him, you turn him down?" Jinn asks. His hair is bed-tousled and falls in front of his eyes.

"Call Lawrence," I say as I toss Jinn my phone. "I'm getting dressed."

"Yes, master," he says. I whirl back around, but see that he's grinning mockingly at me. I toss a stuffed cat at him and slip into the bathroom.

"So, what you're saying is, he'll use me to press Vi, like he used Ollie?" Lawrence asks a few hours later as we sit in the greenhouse at Lawrence's place. I look away, but Jinn gives a serious nod.

"Yes, I think so. You're closest to Viola. He'll use you to get to her. I don't know how—he's good at what he does, it could be anything."

"I'm sorry, Lawr—" I begin desperately, but Lawrence holds up a hand to stop me.

"Don't be. If I can handle coming out to you, Vi, I can handle anything this ifrit can throw at me. Don't wish for me. I don't want you to forget Jinn over me."

Jinn interjects, "It's not that simple, Lawrence. You could get hurt. Physical presses are the most common—"

"What's the alternative, though? She wishes now, when nothing's going on?"

"Well, no, but—" Jinn tries to explain.

"Then leave it. If it gets bad, fine, she wishes me out of it. But not early."

"Lawrence—" I protest again.

"Viola, *stop*," Lawrence replies. He meets my eyes and shakes his head. "Vi, I've always wanted you to be happy. That's why it was so hard for me to tell you . . . to break up with you. So even though it didn't work out with me, I'm not going to get in the way of you being happy again. I'll be fine. If it gets bad, wish for me—but not until it gets bad," he finishes, giving Jinn a firm glance.

I want to speak, but only air escapes my lips—what words are appropriate now? Lawrence reaches forward to touch my hand briefly. At the same moment, Jinn places a soft hand on my shoulder. A broad grin spreads on Lawrence's face as he looks from Jinn's palm to my eyes.

"You should stay near me," Jinn tells Lawrence. "He's less likely to press if I'm around. Too big a risk that I'll interfere or break protocol again by trying to help without Viola using a wish."

"All right. But I'm not sitting in this greenhouse waiting for some angry jinn to make me cry in a rose garden. Let's go somewhere. I'll drive," Lawrence says.

A half hour later we're at the mall, where a traveling carnival has unloaded in the parking lot. It's crowded, despite the fact that the roller coaster looks like it's held together with glue and one of the "rides" is a slide. Little kids with sticky pink cotton candy mouths run around us, and harried mothers look bitter over spending their Sunday counting handfuls of tokens. Lights race around the borders of ride canopies and glint off the sparkly paint of the Ferris wheel, which stretches into the overcast sky. The entire situation seems to make Jinn nervous.

"I can't figure out where they're running to so I can move," he gripes as a small child almost darts right into him.

"So just be visible," Lawrence replies.

"You and Viola are used to seeing me now. You don't realize how unlike a human I look."

He has a good point. His eyes look even more animal-like than usual when the ride lights flicker off them. As we pass the merry-go-round, I glance at our reflections in the gold-framed mirrors that line the center. Even though Jinn walks invisibly just a step behind me and Lawrence, in his place there's a strange and very faint glow in the mirror, a glow you'd never notice were you not looking for it among the dappled plastic horses.

"Do you really think any of these people are looking that closely, Jinn?" Lawrence says.

He has a good point. The mothers are far too occupied reining in their children, the ride operators too interested in convincing the children to ride, and the children too intent on winning stuffed animals. We come to a stop in front of a calliope that's set away from the rides. It plays a charming song that's almost lost to the speakers elsewhere blasting out the local radio station.

"It's a huge breach of the second protocol. Showing myself just to Lawrence is one thing, but to an entire carnival . . . ," Jinn says, his voice wary as he avoids my eyes.

"What if I order you to do it?" I ask, raising an eyebrow. Jinn looks at me.

"Well, I can't really disobey my master," he replies with a sort of smirk.

"I hope you don't think this 'master' thing is going to start working with everyone." Lawrence nudges me playfully. I laugh and am about to turn to Jinn when I see Lawrence's eyes stray very briefly to a boy in the crowd. It's not the first time I've caught him looking at a guy, but it's the first time that I don't care. How could I, when Jinn's eyes are locked on mine?

"Let them see you," I say quietly, looking up at Jinn with a smile. He nods and touches my hand briefly. We step away from the calliope, into the light, with Jinn in full view. The merry-go-round ahead reflects all three of us, a hundred times over.

TWENTY-TWO
Jinn

LATELY, WHENEVER VIOLA gives me a direct order, I'm not sure if I'm obeying because I *have* to or because I *want* to. Like now, when I nod to Viola and instantly shift to become visible to the crowd. A little girl whose face is painted like a tiger walks by and freezes right in front of us, staring at me intensely. I shuffle uncomfortably as she sucks on a piece of her hair, smudging her tiger makeup. Then she smiles—a gummy, six-year-old smile, and scurries away.

I'll be in so much trouble for protocol violations when I get back. They probably won't even bind me to a lamp or bottle. I'll be the Genie of the Toilet Bowl Brush when the

Ancients are through.

But it's worth it. I look at Viola and Lawrence. There's nothing like this in Caliban.

It takes several hours, but my nerves finally fade. Lawrence was right: No one seems to be looking at me too closely, save for the occasional child who notices what the harried mothers don't. Dusk has fallen and the mosquitoes are out. We've ridden most of the rides that we aren't too tall for, so we relax on a periwinkle and seafoam-green picnic table across from a face-painting booth.

"Who is it?" Lawrence asks when Viola's cell phone rings.

"Aaron again," Viola answers, and silences her phone. It's the eighth time he's called since we arrived at the carnival. I catch her eye as she shoves her phone back into her pocket.

"Let's ride the Himalayan again," I suggest, nodding toward the ride.

"Four times? Do they not have cheap carnival rides in Caliban?" Lawrence asks. He looks a little green.

By the time the carnival closes at nightfall, I'm windswept and I smell like sweet popcorn, making me feel extremely mortal. Lawrence drops Viola and me off in her driveway. Just before Viola opens the door, she whirls around and puts a hand on my chest. I freeze under the pressure of her palm, looking into Viola's eyes, afraid that, if I breathe, she'll pull her hand away. Can she feel me changing, aging, the way I could feel her changing?

Viola speaks, blushing. "I just—are you still visible to everyone?" she asks, drawing her hand away. The memory of her hand lingers on my chest for a moment as I raise my eyebrows.

"I forgot," I say, shaking my head. "I can't believe I forgot that. Go ahead, I fixed it." Reverting to invisibility is uncomfortable, like putting on clothes that are too tight, though I'm not sure if it's the act itself or the reminder that I'm not mortal. Viola opens the door.

"Finally! I was worried about you, baby," a voice calls out.

"Um . . . hi," Viola says, stopping in the doorframe. Aaron is sitting at the kitchen counter, magazine in hand. Behind him, Viola's parents watch television; they both turn around to watch as Aaron sets the magazine down and sweeps his hair back.

"You didn't answer my calls all day . . . I got concerned," Aaron says. "I mean, don't think I'm a stalker or something. It just worried me, that's all."

"Right," Viola responds faintly. I wonder what Aaron would do if I were still visible. Aaron wraps an arm around her and kisses her on the cheek. Viola barely moves, so it's like he's hugging a doll. She glances at me, then at her parents, who quickly turn back to the news as if they weren't watching to begin with. Viola pulls away from Aaron, busying herself by shuffling through her purse.

"Well, we're hanging out tomorrow after school, right?" Aaron says, swinging back onto the barstool.

Tomorrow night is the Art Expo.

"I . . . " Viola's voice trails off as she looks at me.

Tell him no, Viola. You don't love him. He doesn't make you whole. He doesn't know you like I do.

I step forward and place my hand on top of hers, and she turns her palm to grasp mine. She exhales.

"I'm busy. I'm sorry."

"Baby, come on, it can wait. Is something wrong?" Aaron

asks, standing. He walks to Viola's side, forcing me to duck out of the way. Viola turns to Aaron and closes her eyes for a moment. When she opens them, she looks at me, standing just behind Aaron's shoulder.

"Nothing's wrong, but I'm busy. It's the Art Expo. I'm sorry," she says, and there's a firmness in her voice that wasn't there before. I smile. Aaron sighs.

"All right. I get it. But here, I brought you these," Aaron says dully. He circles back around the bar and pulls a bouquet of flowers off a bar stool. A dozen yellow and red striped carnations with sprigs of baby's breath.

Striped carnations? I give a quiet laugh. Didn't he bother to learn that striped carnations are for refusal, regret, and bitterness, before he gave them to the girl he loves? Mortal boys are clueless.

But Viola has a sympathetic smile on her lips. Of course. She's always wished someone would bring her flowers. Even if it's Aaron. She takes them from his hand with a look of wonder and pity for Aaron and his efforts.

"I'll see you later, I guess. I love you," Aaron says, and moves to kiss her. Viola starts to step away, but then she glances at the flowers, and a look of guilt passes over her face. She allows him to kiss her cheek, and embraces him quickly.

"Yeah. Thank you," she responds, and Aaron departs, hands shoved in his pockets and a look of defeat on his face.

"I should never have made that wish," Viola mutters to me, her eyes on the floor.

"Was that your new boyfriend?" Viola's mother calls out over the evening news.

"Something like that," Viola answers dully.

Her mother mutes the television and turns around in her chair. "He got here an hour ago and insisted on waiting for you."

"I don't like him," Viola's father adds in a low grumble, without looking at her.

Viola's mother rolls her eyes at her husband and gives Viola a sympathetic look. "I knew the Lawrence thing had you down, but . . . that boy just doesn't seem your type, Vi."

Viola shakes her head and sighs. "He's . . . well, I . . . um . . . I think you may be right." Viola turns to retreat to her bedroom—I linger behind just long enough to see her mother smack her husband's arm and grin at him.

"See? We're reestablishing our relationship with her, just like the book said!"

"Mmm-hmm," her father responds, unmuting the television.

I smirk and shut Viola's door for her, wondering through my amusement if there's a book that could tell me how my relationship with Viola is supposed to work. Do I stay here tonight, with her? Is that the way this works, this longing for each other? Viola vanishes to the bathroom to change. I lean against the windowpane to watch the stars outside.

"Stars?" Viola says, stepping out of the bathroom.

"Exactly," I answer, turning away from the window. I sit down as she combs her hair.

"The Expo is tomorrow afternoon. I still don't know how to explain my paintings," Viola says as she throws back the quilts on her bed. "I started over, you know. Yesterday, before the party, I went to the art room. I painted . . . everything.

Aaron, Lawrence, you, me, Invisible Viola, Shiny Viola, Old Viola . . ."

"What will you say in your speech?" I ask.

"I don't know," she yawns, and sits on the edge of her bed. "I can't talk about painting, period—much less talk about *everything*. No one will understand."

I sit down next to her, keeping a few inches between us. "It doesn't really matter if they understand. It matters that you have the nerve to tell them."

She raises an eyebrow at me. "You've never actually been to high school, have you?"

THE NEXT MORNING, I don't sleep in Shakespeare class. Instead, I spend the time poring over my Expo speech. It's not very good. Actually, it sucks. It doesn't even make sense; it's all a jumble of names and feelings and types of people and . . . stupidity. I really shouldn't have started over. I should've stuck with my boring forest paintings. I work on my speech in every class that follows, and I skip lunch to try and hunt down a the-saurus. But before I've written even a full paragraph, the final bell is ringing, and I'm ducking into the art room, just hours away from the start of the Expo.

"Hello, stranger," a cheery voice calls out as I pull the art room door shut. I almost shout in surprise, and wheel around toward the speaker.

It's Ollie. But she doesn't look like Ollie. Not the Ollie that I longed to be *or* the sobbing Ollie from the garden. She's not wearing much makeup, and though she's still draped in beautiful thrift store finds, they're not as tight and don't match as perfectly. She even seems to have gained a little weight, but looks all the better for it.

"Ollie! Hi!" I finally reply, after Ollie has already turned back to the painting she's touching up. She's adding more bright pink to an armchair in a forest.

"I saw your Expo paintings lying on the table," Ollie says, pointing to the forest pieces. "You aren't backing out, are you?" she continues.

"No, no, I just . . . I started over," I explain sheepishly. Looking at my original paintings, I feel a little like I'm seeing old photos of myself. "I haven't really shown them to anyone. They were sort of a last-minute inspiration. They don't even fit the landscape theme."

"Yeah, well, the theme sucks," Ollie says with a laugh. "Can

I see them?" She steps closer; she smells of clean linen and lavender.

For a moment, Invisible Viola returns, and I want to stammer about how much better Ollie's pieces are than mine. It's true. But it doesn't matter. Not anymore, really. Ollie is just a girl, just a . . . a friend? I don't need to study her like I used to, to try and figure out how to belong in her crowd. She's a better painter, yes. But at least now my pieces are my own, not attempts at being Ollie, or at being punk or emo or popular. I nod and pull the covers off my paintings.

The paintings are sort of a mess. People with blurry faces, defined by their hair and clothes and the colors that surround their fuzzy forms. Scenes from parties, from school, the backs of heads in classes and the dark, small forms of Invisible Girls.

"Oh, wow," Ollie says sincerely. She smiles and nods as she studies each one carefully. Once she passes over the fifth and final painting, she meets my eyes again. "These are amazing."

"Well, the technique is kind of rushed . . . ," I mumble through a grin.

"Yeah, but the originality! And the emotion, they're . . .

they're powerful," Ollie says. "I was afraid you'd get distracted. It's what happened to me when I dated Aaron. I mean, he's a good guy and all, but painting isn't really something he's too focused on. I don't know. It's like he and I were meant to be together because we ran in the same circles, but we didn't bother to think about whether we had the feelings that come with 'meant to be together.' If that makes sense. Which I don't think it does." Ollie says, tossing her hair back. "It's just easier now, I'm more . . . more me. And I'm dating again anyhow," she finishes with a slight blush.

"Really? Who?"

"Xander Davis."

"Wow" is all I can think to say. Xander Davis is nothing like Aaron. He's a staple in the school's darkroom and master of the photography department, though he's known more for his spiky blue hair than for his photos. He's on my level. Well, my old level, I realize, thinking of the high-school social order. He was someone I could have dated, even when I was Invisible Viola.

"Yeah. He sees me. Aaron didn't. Maybe Aaron sees you,

though," Ollie says with a friendly shrug.

Not hardly. A boy with blue hair appears at the door—Xander.

"Ophelia?" he says, and his voice sounds poetic, like he's speaking the lyrics of a song. Ollie grins.

"You said you wouldn't call me that in public, *Lysander,*" she teases him back.

"Wait—*Ophelia*?" I ask in surprise as I set up a blank canvas.

"It's my first name. I think I may go back to it for a while instead of *Ollie.*"

"It's a beautiful name," I say.

"Hey—it's Viola, right?" Xander says, and there's still a tone of poetry in his voice. "We're grabbing dinner before the Expo tonight. You want anything?"

"Me? No. No, I'm good. Thank you, though." I say quickly. "I've got to figure out a way to tie all this into the whole landscape thing."

Ollie furrows her eyebrows. "Hmm . . . you could do . . . human landscapes? No—social landscapes, maybe?"

Social landscapes. "That's perfect," I say. "Thank you."

"No problem. Give me a call if you change your mind about dinner," Ollie says as she washes her hands in the sink. She nods at me as she slips her hand into Xander's, and then they vanish into the hallway.

"She looks different. But good," a soft voice says. I turn to see Jinn leaning against a table. His dark eyes glimmer, and in the silence he brushes several black curls from his face. How was I ever scared of him? And now all I want is for him to be closer to me. I flush, because I know he can read the desire in me. He looks at my paintings closely, studying them silently for several minutes, until a small but warm smile crosses his lips. He doesn't say anything. But he doesn't really need to.

He turns to me, black curls in his eyes. "Can I help you set up?"

Jinn helps me set up my easels and exhibit in the theater lobby. We don't talk, really, just a series of warm glances and slight touches that make my head buzz. We laugh when a passerby catches me seemingly talking to myself, and I lay a few hurried last brushstrokes on my pieces. Lawrence shows up early, and the other two students in the Expo have also arrived. One is trailed by her parents, who are swarming around her like wasps; the other is weeping hysterically in his mother's arms.

I'm still Aaron Moor's Girlfriend, Shiny Viola, as far as the Royal Family is concerned—a fact I almost managed to forget until they show up all at once, laughing and talking. I play nice—I hug Aaron but dodge the kiss he tries to give me, and I compliment the shiny girls on their new highlights and lime-green skirts. But then I cling to Lawrence, Ollie, Xander, and—though no one but Lawrence and I see him—Jinn. We sit on a bench together, waiting for the presentations to start. Ollie and Xander eat Thai food, and Lawrence cracks jokes about the cast of *Grease*.

The Expo starts slowly—Sarah Larson, the girl with the wasp-parents, is muddling through her speech when my parents arrive. My parents wave and whisper my name loudly enough that my face reddens. Lawrence rises and motions them over to stand by him. I force my eyes down to my notebook paper, which, save for some scattered thoughts, is pretty much useless.

What am I going to say? How can I talk to these people about the things I painted, especially now that all my paintings are about *them*, really? About watching them, about how they exclude and include people by some crazy formula that no one really seems to know. How can I try and explain about needing to belong in order to feel whole . . . ?

Sarah finishes her speech, quivering as she runs a hand through her choppy black hair and leaves the stage. My knees shake, but I stand slowly and see that Jinn is standing beside Lawrence, his eyes locked on mine in the intense way that scared me so badly the first time I saw him.

I can do this. I can talk about painting, about what it really means. I don't need to hide behind artwork anymore. I can do this.

As long as I don't pass out.

I rise and walk to the podium. A few people cough. A little kid in the front picks his nose. I forget to introduce myself.

"The topic was landscapes," I start slowly, looking at the sparse outline of my speech. *Look at Jinn, just look at Jinn.* "And at first I painted trees and forests and stuff, but, honestly, I don't care about those landscapes. Painting them didn't do anything for me on a more . . . *passionate* level. So I started over, and I painted something else. I painted social landscapes. About what it's like to be on both ends from either perspective: what it's like to be invisible and what it's like to be in love and feel all shiny. About all the parts of a person that make them belong . . . or make them feel alone."

I pause—Lawrence is whispering something to Jinn. Jinn laughs and nods back. Lawrence tugs on my dad's arm and motions toward Jinn, who smiles and extends a hand to both my parents. He's fully visible.

I suppress a grin and add, "My pieces are about how important it is to be seen. And they're also really technically sloppy. Sorry." The crowd laughs with me, and a few of the other art students nod in agreement. Aaron checks his watch. My mom casts Jinn a stern look, studying him carefully.

And that's it. The speech is over—shorter than everyone else's, but that's all I needed to say. All I wanted to say. Ollie passes me on her way to the podium and squeezes my arm gently. When I've stepped down, Xander nods and gives me a thumbs-up. My parents, Lawrence, and Jinn work their way over to where I'm standing.

"We met your friend Jinn," my mother whispers to me.

"I saw," I respond. "I like him better than Aaron. What do you and Dad think?"

My mom glances back at Jinn. "I am supportive of your relationship," she says like it's a prerecorded line. She shrugs. "And hey, at least he isn't gay."

I nod back at her and laugh under my breath, because, finally, I think it's funny.

TWENTY-FOUR

Jinn

"SO I'VE MADE it through another day without the jinn police coming after me," Lawrence comments over pizza. It's Friday, and the stars overhead are visible through the greenhouse roof. For the first time, I like this room. Viola is sitting on the floor; Lawrence sprawls across one couch as I slowly sink into the other.

"We still shouldn't go out. Getting in a car is practically asking for a car wreck press," I say.

"These ifrit guys sound brutal," Lawrence notes. He's trying to sound casual, but there's the smallest hint of fear in his voice.

"As long as we can keep you physically safe, you'll be fine," I say in what I hope is a comforting voice. Lawrence doesn't seem totally convinced.

Viola's cell phone rings again. Aaron. Not surprising. He's been calling since we slunk out of the Expo, avoiding him. I have to feel a little sorry for him—I did quite a job when I granted Viola's wish for his love. Poor guy's heart must be breaking that she's ignoring him.

"Maybe you should just answer it," Lawrence says in annoyance. There's a party tonight, according to Lawrence, that a college-age friend of Aaron's is throwing. Both Lawrence and Viola are supposed to be there, but neither wanted to go—I'm not sure whether it's because of the impending press or because they're just sick of football players and beer.

This is what I'll miss, I think as I watch Viola and Lawrence bicker over answering the phone. So casual, so lighthearted, even though Lawrence is risking everything just so she can be happy. So I can be happy. Mortal relationships—this is what makes them beautiful. How can I go back to Caliban after this? Jinn relationships don't compare—I presume that this is our legendary punishment.

Viola gives in and answers the phone, then vanishes to another room.

"I didn't think I'd ever feel this sorry for Aaron Moor," Lawrence says as he watches her go.

"He loves her. He thinks she makes him whole. It's got to be hard for him just to let her go," I answer, my voice low and eyes down.

"Well. The course of true love never did run smoothly, I suppose," Lawrence answers, though it's not clear if he's speaking on Aaron's behalf or mine. Either way, I agree.

"I was thinking," Lawrence says, glancing down. "Viola summoned you by having a strong wish, right? Something huge. Then you got sort of . . . assigned to her?"

I nod. How long ago was that?

"Okay, so what if, after she makes the final wish, I figure out some way to wish or . . . you figure out some way to reassign yourself to her. Could you come back?"

I smile. "Viola can't summon me because she's already been my master. That's why she forgets me—the third wish severs the connection between Viola and me. And even if you did manage to summon me, what then? Viola will have forgotten about me already. So I grant your wishes and vanish again, then you *both* will have forgotten me. I don't want that for you any more than I want it for Viola."

But I appreciate the effort more than I know how to say.

"I could hold off on wishing—" Lawrence attempts.

"So that they use Viola to press you?" I ask. Lawrence sighs in defeat as Viola returns to the room, a look of annoyance on her face.

"Aaron has to have gotten the message now," Viola says, tossing her phone on the coffee table and glaring at it. She drops to the floor, legs folded beneath her.

"I dunno," Lawrence answers. "Guys are pretty dense."

Viola nods and leans back against my knees, the tips of her ears turning the faintest shade of carnation pink when our eyes meet. I touch her hair lightly as Lawrence collects our empty dinner plates.

"We should do something. I can't just sit around waiting for evil genies to make me cry," Lawrence calls as he makes his way to the kitchen. As he begins to bang around, rinsing dishes, Viola turns to face me.

"Is it safe? I mean, for us to go out with the . . . ifrit out there?" She says *ifrit* like the word itself frightens her, and I try to make my smile reassuring.

"It doesn't matter where we are, really. We're just as safe out there as in here. We could go to your party, if that's what you want."

Viola wrinkles her nose and shakes her head. "Not a chance."

"What about this?" Lawrence asks, reappearing in the kitchen doorway with a half-eaten bag of jumbo marshmallows and a box of sparklers. I raise my eyebrows, and Viola laughs.

"We haven't done that since . . . well, since we were dating," she says.

Lawrence looks uncomfortable for a glimmer of a moment, but his expression fades into a grin when Viola stands and offers me a hand to do the same. Lawrence opens the back door, and Viola ushers me forward silently.

Lawrence's backyard is filled with faded gnome statues

and trees surrounded by little wire borders. The smell of cut grass hangs heavily in the air, and we walk along a tiny, worn path until we reach the border of the yard. It's dark, but a few streetlights shine through the trees and I can make out a wooden fence on the edge of the property. There's a shallow fire pit that I can barely see; Lawrence and Viola drop down into the pine straw on either side. I sit beside Viola as Lawrence rips through the sparkler packaging. He removes three like he's drawing a sword and leans to hand the rest to me.

"I forgot to grab a lighter," Lawrence says as I take three sparklers, rolling them between my fingers.

"I'll go get it," Viola says as she withdraws her own sparklers. The space next to me feels uncomfortably empty as she begins to walk away.

"Wait," I say, holding up a hand to stop her. "I'll get it." I beckon for her to lower her sparklers and place my fingertips on the top of a crimson tinted one. My fingers heat up and glow orange, until her sparkler kicks to life in a spray of red and gold. Viola smiles and touches my head lightly as she lights one of my sparklers off hers.

"Yeah, yeah," Lawrence says over the hiss of sulfur and charcoal burning. "But can you manage a campfire, Prometheus?"

I laugh and point my sparkler toward the fire pit like it's a wand, and a few dry leaves smoke, then crinkle to life somewhat undramatically. Lawrence pulls several logs and broken furniture pieces from a covered pile behind him, and soon a tiny fire is crackling, casting our faces in a dull orange glow. Viola's eyes flicker in the darkness, and she tosses her finished sparkler into the flames, moving closer to me as she does so. Lawrence catches my eyes and smiles a little before opening the bag of marshmallows.

"So this is how it works," Lawrence explains to me. "You light a sparkler and write something in the air with it."

"A secret," Viola corrects him. "It doesn't have to be a big secret or anything, just . . . a secret. Preferably a short one."

"Right," Lawrence continues. "So you write it in the air with the sparkler, and whoever can guess it first gets a marshmallow to roast."

"I should add that we invented this game when we were about eight years old—" Viola begins.

"No," I interrupt and grin. "No, I like the sound of it. Besides, I can read you both, which probably means I'll get most of the marshmallows anyway."

They laugh together like this hadn't occurred to them, and then Lawrence touches the tip of a sparkler to the fire. It ignites in a shower of neon green and he leans forward, swirling it in the air like an orchestra conductor. The fire blazes stronger as the sawed off legs of an old chair catch the flames.

"I told," Viola spells out Lawrence's first two words. He writes the phrase again. For a moment, I try to read Lawrence's wishes instead of the sparkler, but it somehow feels intrusive and I quickly turn back to the green trail of light.

"Mother? Your mother?" I guess at the next two words. Lawrence nods and writes the final part again as the sparkler threatens to burn up.

"You told your mom you're gay!" Viola nearly shouts in disbelief.

Lawrence laughs and tosses her a marshmallow, which she sticks on a bent-up wire coat hanger and thrusts into the fire. "This morning," Lawrence explains. "It didn't go so well, but it's better than all the hiding, I guess. But if she sends me to one of those gay-reform schools, you'd better use those Prometheus powers to break me out, Jinn," he finishes, grinning.

Viola laughs as her marshmallow burns and the outside crinkles like paper; she pulls it from the fire, blows on the charred section, and delicately pulls it off the hanger. She gives Lawrence a long look, but remains silent; I get the impression she doesn't need to say she's proud—he understands.

"Your turn, Vi," Lawrence breaks the quiet. Viola swallows the marshmallow, and then holds the end of her sparkler in the fire until it crackles and ignites.

Her letters are more deliberate than Lawrence's, like she's trying to read her own words just as we are. She looks through the violet swirls to meet my eyes meaningfully, and her lips part, like she wants to break the rules of the game and tell me. I immediately know what she's writing, but not because I'm actively trying to read her; I just see her so clearly, somehow. Like I've known her for ages.

"You broke up with Aaron," I say, trying to calm the smile that yanks at the corners of my mouth.

"That's not a secret," Lawrence complains, and throws a marshmallow at Viola.

"Yes, it is!" Viola answers as the marshmallow rolls into the fire. "I mean, you knew I was going to, I'm sure, but . . . I actually just told him it's over. I wanted you both to know before . . . *if* Jinn leaves."

I nod and gaze into the fire. It's selfish, really, but knowing she isn't with Aaron anymore is comforting; the magic binding him to her will quickly fade. I'd wondered how long Viola would be able to resist Aaron's "charms" after she forgot about me, and us, and . . . everything. It's hard to ignore the kind of devotion a wish can create.

I refuse the marshmallow Lawrence offers me, and instead light one of my sparklers with my fingertips, without ever looking away from Viola. I write the words over and over in bright blue script. Viola's eyes follow my hand, then shine in comprehension.

"I w—," she begins to translate the secret, but stops herself short, clamping a hand over her mouth.

"Wait, what?" Lawrence asks. I laugh and turn the sparkler

toward him. It takes only two repetitions till he understands the secret Viola couldn't say aloud.

"I wish I were human," Lawrence translates for me. I nod and toss the sparkler in the fire. Lawrence smiles and puts a marshmallow on a hanger for himself.

"Not fair. I guessed it first," Viola pretends to complain.

"Yeah, but that wasn't a real secret either," complains Lawrence. "You both suck at this game."

"You're just mad because you're going to gay-reform school," Viola teases. Lawrence eats his marshmallows melodramatically, until Viola jumps up and snatches the bag from beside him. Lawrence is quick to lunge toward her in response, and I have to pull my legs in to avoid tripping them as they clumsily chase each other around the campfire. Viola pauses to toss a handful of marshmallows back at Lawrence, and when she's concentrating on her aim, I snatch the bag out of her hand and hold it behind my back.

"Who's got the power now?" I grin as I stand up and peg both of them with marshmallows.

"You," Lawrence says, dropping his hands. "I'm pretty

positive you can kick my ass."

"Me," Viola snickers. "Don't think I'm above giving you a direct order if it means winning the marshmallow war."

"You wouldn't," I say, stepping closer to her and trying to hide my smile. She comes up only to my shoulders, but she narrows her eyes in a poor attempt to look stern. I laugh and become invisible, stepping out of her reach as she snatches at the now empty air before her.

"Wish for the bag back, Vi," Lawrence urges her, eyes darting around as if I'll sneak up on him. "There's more mythological men where he comes from."

Viola laughs and folds her arms. "All right, fine. Jinn wins," she says in a mocking tone, then drops back to the ground. "But you're lucky I like you more than marshmallows, or you'd already be gone." I grin and reappear just behind Viola's shoulder, then toss the bag back to Lawrence. Viola turns to give me a fake exasperated look, her hair falling carelessly in front of her eyes in a way that's completely unlike a female jinn. "Stupid no-mermaid rules," she mutters, eyes glittering.

"I agree," I answer. Viola leans in to warm her hands by the fire.

"Are you cold?" I ask. She nods, and I hold up a hand, ready to conjure a blanket.

"Wait," Lawrence says. "I'll go get one for you from the house. I need something to drink after that marshmallow feast anyway."

"I can do that, too," I say, holding up my other hand.

"No." Lawrence stops me. "I don't care what superpowers you have. My mother's tendency toward homophobia aside, she makes amazing sweet tea that no one can duplicate."

"I'll go," I say—somehow, I feel a little noble for taking care of her. Stupid, I know, but I like the feeling.

"Really? Thanks. There's a blanket by the door," Lawrence says.

I brush myself off and walk back to the greenhouse. Viola laughs—the deep laugh that she never used with Aaron. It's soothing, like a medication for the worry of a final wish, and I hesitate to shut the greenhouse door behind me, waiting for the laughter to end. I grab the nearest afghan, which is imprinted with the image of a cocker spaniel puppy, and turn toward the kitchen for Lawrence's drink.

"I'm so sorry, my friend."

I know the voice. Each syllable is an elegantly enunciated sound. I hate the voice. It reaches into me and strangles the warmth that Viola created, destroys the hope for more time with her. I drop the cocker spaniel blanket and turn around.

His eyes are dark, and his mouth is curved into a hard grimace. The silk tunic is abnormal and strange in Lawrence's living room, and I have to fight the urge to pointlessly shout for him to get away from here, from me, from her. The ifrit's eyes travel from mine to the greenhouse window, to the fireside. My breathing halts as I see Lawrence's head snap toward me, his eyes full of desperation and unwillingness, silently begging me for help.

TWENTY-FIVE

Viola

THE STARS ABOVE me aren't as bright as the ones I remember from the night in the garden with Ollie. They're the same stars, I know, but still . . . I suppose it's just the wispy layer of clouds between me and them. The fire crackles loudly, and I look back to Lawrence, waiting for him to finish the story he was telling.

"Lawrence?" I say slowly. He seems to be in some sort of daze. His eyes are dim like the stars, and the bright smile is gone, his square jaw set in a firm line. I wave my hand to get his attention, laughing at his expression. He doesn't respond.

"Um . . . Laurie?" I call his baby name, which always used

to get a reaction out of him when we were dating. I glance back at his house, hoping to see Jinn walking toward us, but no. We're alone.

"Vi—," he finally says in an urgent tone, like he's trying to announce something immensely important. He cuts himself off, and his cheeks flush as he shakes his head and mutters to himself. He rubs his palms together, and I can see droplets of sweat forming on his forehead. This isn't like Lawrence—he's never looked nervous, except for the day we broke up. He's the one who's supposed to be reliably calm and collected. My nerves spike.

"Is something wrong?" I ask. "Wait, you didn't get stung by a bee, did you? I know where the EpiPen is—" I jump to my feet, ready to run into the house and wondering how long someone highly allergic to bees can last if stung. I've taken only a single step when Lawrence shakes his head and holds up a hand to stop me.

"Lawrence," I say testily. "Tell me what's wrong."

Lawrence runs a hand through his hair, tousling it out of its hairstylist-perfect glory, then eases his head into his hands as if in pain. I drop to my knees beside him, and dampness from the cold dirt soaks into my jeans. I put a hand on his shoulder.

"Vi . . . I have to tell you. . . . Viola . . . ," he mutters into his fists mournfully.

"Lawrence, please," I say through the weight of worry that's swelling in my throat.

"Okay," he says breathily. "Okay. I have to tell you." Keeping his head down, he gently tugs my hand off his shoulder and encases it in his sweaty palms. He runs his thumb across the tips of my fingers delicately, then brings my hand to his lips and kisses it softly. My hand jerks uncomfortably when his lips touch my skin, and I can't hide the grimace that crosses my face. I yank my hand away and furrow my eyebrows. Lawrence's head snaps up, and he watches me hide my hand behind my back, before his eyes rise to meet mine.

"Vi, love . . . I made a mistake. I made a horrible mistake," he whispers, eyes wide and scared.

"What mistake?" I say hollowly. I can still feel where his lips touched my hand, but it's strange and it makes me want to brush the sensation away. This is Lawrence. He's my best friend;

he isn't supposed to kiss my hand, to look at me the way he's looking at me now. I fold my arms across my chest and sit back on my heels.

He says the words like they're a poem he's memorized, some long-practiced speech full of words that he's frightened he'll forget. "I love you, Vi. I've never stopped loving you."

I stop breathing.

His eyes are watery with pain when my body tenses at his words; words that I dreamed of him saying almost every night following our breakup. He reaches forward and runs his fingers through my hair gently, letting the back of his hand brush against my cheek. Lawrence's breath shakes in what I think is either fear or desire. I want to pull away, but there's a pain in his eyes that locks me in place. I dig my fingers into the dirt in confusion and try to force myself to stand, but it's pointless.

A sharp bang sounds from the greenhouse, and I finally gasp like I'm surfacing for air. Lawrence and I both turn, nearly bumping our heads together we're so close. It's Jinn, standing in the open doorway. The door slams against the house again with the breeze. His eyes meet mine, pulling my gaze into him in a way I'd find dazzling were it not for the sadness behind them. And in that single glance, I understand.

The press. This is the press.

Lawrence turns my face back toward him and wraps his arms around me, pulling me to him and pressing his lips to mine so quickly that I don't even realize we're kissing at first. His lips move quickly, gently but more eager than I remember, and I cry out as best as I can, his strong arms holding me fast to him. I weasel my hands to his shoulders and try to push away, but he pulls me even closer into the fold of his arms, the very place I spent so many hours longing to return but now just want to escape from. This isn't how I thought it was, isn't how I ever wanted it to be . . . and isn't who I want to be kissing. I press my lips together to try and stop the kiss. *Jinn, please help me escape, please fix this . . . please, I wish—*

No. I don't wish. The word *wish* sticks in my mind and creates a fear that gives me newfound power. I force Lawrence from me with a sharp cry, leaping to my feet and sending him backward into the dead leaves that cover the ground.

"No," I say under my breath, as if saying the word will give me strength. No wishes. I can't—if I do, it'll be the last. The good-bye wish. The wind changes directions, and the campfire smoke swirls around me until my eyes burn.

"Please, Viola," Lawrence groans, rubbing the back of his head where it struck the ground. I look over at Jinn. He's breathing heavily, silhouetted in the greenhouse door. He balls his hands into fists and suddenly sprints toward me. I want to hold out my arms, I want him to embrace me. But no—he has to stay out of this. I can fix this without involving him, without involving a wish. I *have* to fix this without a wish. I swallow hard and command myself to speak just as the fire's orange glow begins to glint off his tawny skin.

"No! Don't come any closer!" A direct order. I hate myself for giving it, and my chest aches like a knife is cutting through me. Jinn freezes in place and stares at me, pleading silently. I shake my head and look away as Jinn fights the hold, trying to lift his feet and take another step while cursing under his breath. I turn to Lawrence and try to summon some amount of courage.

"Lawrence, this isn't you," I say hoarsely. "Stop it."

Lawrence shakes his head and tries to stand, but dizzily sits back in the dirt, rubbing the back of his head again. He grimaces in pain but finally speaks. "Viola, this is more me than I've been in months. You have to believe me. I can't do this anymore; I can't be without you. Please."

"This isn't you," I repeat, but my voice shakes and my legs feel too heavy to move away. Lawrence grabs hold of a tree trunk and pulls himself to standing—my instinct is to rush in and help support his weight, but I'm afraid to. Lawrence slowly raises his head and releases the birch tree, taking a shaky step toward me. I'm about to step away when he suddenly pitches forward, and before I can overanalyze I reach out for him, worried that he'll topple into the fire if I don't help.

Lawrence both falls against me and pulls me into his arms at once, like we're trapped in some strange and somewhat familiar dance. He finds his balance and I'm no longer helping him stand, but rather we're simply holding each other. He rests his chin on my head as if we're reuniting after ages apart, and he sighs, sounding so relieved that I can't muster the strength to push him away, to hurt him, or to beg him to stop. At least, I can't do it without making a wish. I hold my breath to stop a sob from escaping my throat.

TWENTY-SIX
Jinn

I LOOK AWAY as Lawrence and Viola embrace. My stomach lurches and I tremble. I try to take a step forward, to run to her, but her order for me to stay away locks my feet in place. I have to get to her, I have to help her. . . . I roar into the night, staring angrily at my feet. When I look back up, my heart leaps in anger.

The ifrit stands on the opposite side of the campfire, looking eerie and dark in the firelight. The flames reflect off his tunic and make him look older than ever, defining the strong line of his chin and the hollows of his cheeks. I lunge toward Viola, but the force holding my feet in place causes me to fall to the ground, slamming my chest into the layer of dead leaves. I hear Viola begin to sob, and when I look up, she's pushing away from him gently. She wipes tears from her eyes and backs up into a massive oak tree, reaching behind her to grasp it, as if its thick branches can protect her. Lawrence looks crushed and follows her gaze toward me.

"Is this because of him?" Lawrence asks, looking between me and Viola. His eyes are filled with aching desire and anger—he doesn't even look like the Lawrence I know. "You're looking at him . . . Viola, you're looking at him the way you used to look at me. Don't, please don't . . ."

"Lawrence, I just—" Viola begins, but Lawrence stomps toward me, breathing heavily.

"He can't love you like I can, Vi. He's not even human," he pleads. "But, Vi, we can have the love story. The epic love story you always wanted."

"But this isn't real," Viola says in a whisper. I'm not sure if she's telling Lawrence or herself.

Lawrence turns to glare at me. "It's because of you. You showed up and ruined everything."

"Lawrence, listen to yourself," I say firmly, taking a step away from him. His eyes flash with some semblance of old Lawrence. He's fighting the press. He'll lose, but he's fighting it—the ifrit shifts awkwardly on the other side of the campfire. I press my lips together as Lawrence balls his fists and takes another step toward me.

"It's your fault. You can't love her like I can, you *jinn!*" he shouts, then lunges toward me. Viola cries out and begins to sob. Lawrence's first punch makes contact with my head and sends a ripping pain through my ear and jaw. I fall back against the nearest tree and hold my hands out toward him. He's strong— very strong, actually—and shoves through my hands to sink another fist into my stomach. It feels like every ounce of air is being forced from my lungs, and I fall to my knees coughing.

I try to say his name again, but I can't even catch my breath to speak. In his shadow, I see him raising his arm again. I turn just in time to catch his wrist and yank him to the ground.

"I'm not fighting you, Lawrence. You're my friend," I say raspily as Lawrence springs back to his feet. I close my eyes, waiting for more pain. I know I won't be able to hit him back.

Yet I can't leave—for Viola's sake *and* for Lawrence's.

I have the power to grant the wishes of others, but right now I'm helpless.

Suddenly Viola rushes forward, between Lawrence and me. She puts her hands on Lawrence's chest and urges him backward, shaking her head frantically. There's a look of determination on her tearstained face.

"Did you hear that, Vi? He won't even fight for you. I'll fight for you. I'll do anything for you."

"Stop it, Lawrence. Please stop it," she commands, her voice wavering the smallest bit. I stand and wince in pain, causing the ifrit to shake his head in disappointment. I grit my teeth and look back to Viola. Lawrence's hands lie gently on her cheeks, and he brushes her tears away with his thumbs.

"Vi, please. I never meant to hurt you, but . . . I had to tell you. I love you, Vi," he whispers, grasping toward her. She chokes on a sob.

"No, Lawrence. You're my best friend," Viola pleads, her determination fading. "I don't want to hurt you. This isn't you. Don't make me do this."

"Make it stop!" I shout at the ifrit. Lawrence doesn't seem to hear me—I'm not sure if it's because of his fixation on Viola or because of something the ifrit is doing.

"This is what she wanted," the ifrit responds, his face sad and grim. Viola whirls around and sees him for the first time. She shrinks backward and folds her arms over her chest, stepping away from the ifrit and Lawrence at the same time. The ifrit continues, ignoring her, "This is what she wanted before you came here, before you broke protocol and meddled in her life. This will make her happy."

"Look at her! She isn't happy! She doesn't want this anymore!" I scream at him. "Vi, don't do it. Don't wish, this isn't real. You can walk away from him."

"Come on, Vi," Lawrence says softly. "Just one more chance." His voice is gentle and convincing. Am I losing her? Is it working?

I raise my hand toward her, aching to move closer, to take her in my arms like Lawrence did, but her order prevents me from budging. "You don't have to wish, Viola."

"You don't have to wish," the ifrit tells Viola, "but then

this won't end." Viola turns toward him, a breeze casting her hair around her scared face. I want to stand between her and the ifrit, but she won't let me move. She steps toward the ifrit, trembling.

"It has to end," she says in a faint whisper. "This isn't Lawrence."

"No," the ifrit agrees.

"But I can't lose Jinn," she continues, her voice high-pitched as tears spill from her eyes.

"He is a jinn. You're a human. Your lives are incompatible—if it didn't end now, it would just end badly later. There are only two ways to stop it. You can wish for the press to stop. The boy will go back to normal, and the jinn will return home."

Viola looks to Lawrence, then back to the ifrit, who continues, his voice careful and guarded. "Or you can just wish for the jinn to return home."

"I won't," Viola says fiercely, leaving the safety of the tree trunk and stomping closer to the ifrit. The tone of her voice drenches me in an odd sort of relief; she still wants me.

"You should," the ifrit says gently. "You will forget about the jinn either way. But if you wish for him to go, the boy will still want you after the jinn is gone. You'll have the love you wanted so badly to begin with."

"But it won't be real," she murmurs, shaking her head and backing away from him. "That's not how it works. I can't just wish for love like that. I've tried it. It doesn't work."

"It didn't work only because of the jinn," the ifrit says calmly. "And once he's gone, you won't know that it isn't real." Viola and the ifrit stare at each other for a long time, despite the fact that both Lawrence and I call Viola's name. Viola turns toward Lawrence.

"Viola!" I shout. "Don't listen to him! Look at me, please," I shout, but Viola doesn't listen—she takes a step closer to Lawrence. I turn my glare to the ifrit.

"Don't do this to her. You're supposed to be my friend," I growl.

"That's *why* I'm doing it. My job is to save your life, even if you don't want to be saved. Don't be so selfish. She'll forget you either way. Would you prefer the girl to go on unloved and unhappy or to finally have the boy? You know him by now; you know he'll love her just as much as you do."

"She doesn't have to wish!" I snarl. "It's her choice, not yours."

"True," the ifrit agrees. "But it's just a matter of time. And you know how this works—I'll press her again and again, and the presses will only get worse. It's my job—I can't change that. Don't make her suffer just so you can be happy."

"So *we* can be . . . ," I start, but I have to look away when my tongue feels heavy in my throat and I can't speak.

The ifrit continues, "If you love her, you'll tell her to wish for you to go. She'll be happy. I performed this press as if it were a wish—he truly loves her. You know she'll be happy. *Jinn.*"

The word doesn't sound like my name when the ifrit says it. Something is missing from it, some sort of warmth. I turn toward Viola and am almost surprised when I realize her eyes are on me. We don't speak, but I get the impression neither of us knows what to say. She bites her lip and takes half a step away from the firelight, toward me. I want her to release the hold on me, to let me go, but somehow—even without looking for wishes in her eyes—I know she won't. She's too afraid. Viola glances at Lawrence. He's edged his way closer to her, his eyes full of sincerity and longing.

The ifrit sighs at me. "Stop this, jinn. How long can you let this continue? Another hour? A week? A year? It has to end at some point. How long will you let her be in pain before you allow her to end it?"

"She doesn't want me to go," I say, so quietly I can barely hear my own voice. Viola doesn't flinch away when Lawrence reaches forward and lets his fingertips rest on her arm.

"Don't be selfish. You know this can end only one way."

No, no. Please, no! I shout to myself. But there's a second voice in my head that whispers, *Yes. Lawrence will love her in a way no other mortal could. He's the only one you can trust to love her, if it can't be you.*

I look at Lawrence mournfully, but his eyes are locked on Viola, full of adoration and pain. She'll forget me. I can't stop that. But she could be happy. Without me, she could be happy. The ifrit is right—how many presses will I make her go through? What pain will she have to endure just so we can have a few more moments together? I inhale, and although I try to say the words, I can't form the sounds in my mouth.

Wish, Viola.

Wish for him. I'm making the choice for you. Just wish for him.

Viola snaps her head toward me, as if she could hear my thoughts. I shake my head at her and stop fighting her hold on me.

"Viola, wish! This has to end. Wish for me to go," I say, trying to force a calm tone that isn't terribly convincing. The fire sputters, clinging desperately to the last few scraps of fuel.

"But I'll forget you," she whispers, eyes firmly on mine. Lawrence begins to draw her closer again, wrapping an arm around her waist and brushing her hair from her face with his free hand. He loves her, but she doesn't look away from me.

"You'll forget me in the end either way," I say numbly. "But this way you can at least be happy." I close my eyes and turn my head away—maybe if she doesn't have to look at me, it'll be easier. "Do it, Viola."

"I can't."

"You can. Wish me gone."

"It won't be Lawrence anyway, and I won't have you—"

"Vi, if you love me the way I love you, wish for me to go," I plead, an almost threatening sound in my voice. I look back up to find Viola's eyes on mine, an intense stare, like she's trying to read something in me. I realize that somehow, in the middle of all this, the fact that I love her has slipped out. I love her. Why didn't I tell her before now? The hollow feeling in my chest expands until I feel like I might drown from it.

Lawrence cups her face in his hand and turns her gaze to him. He exhales, then leans in, pressing his lips against hers like she's the only person he ever intends to kiss for the rest of his life. And she kisses him back.

Do it. Please. Wish. Viola pulls out of the kiss and sighs softly, looking Lawrence in the eye.

"Please," I say under my breath. *Please.*

Her gaze turns to me, eyes bright and watery in the firelight. "I love you," she whispers.

A small cry escapes my lips, and I can't breathe—my chest feels like a sieve, being filled with warmth that's so quickly slipping away. . . . I force myself to swallow.

Please, Viola. Go. Be happy. Love Lawrence, since I won't be here for you to love me.

She inhales and closes her eyes. "I wish the press to be taken off Lawrence."

Her voice is so tiny and small that I almost don't hear it, but the pull of the wish rips at me like a dam being released. This is the wrong wish, this isn't what she was supposed to say, yet some part of me wants to both cry and shout in happiness—she wanted me, *me*, not Lawrence, not a jinn, but *me*. The force of the magic drags me under itself, and I struggle to keep it from running wild. The last wish. It's through, and I can't stop it or change it. I jerk backward in pain as the magic pulls at me, and I have to say it before the power overtakes me. I part my lips, and the words slip out in a forced whisper.

"As you wish."

TWENTY-SEVEN

Viola

I EXHALE AND open my eyes. Something feels wrong, but I can't pinpoint it—it's as if I've just woken up from a nap and am still too groggy to truly understand where I am. The campfire sputters in front of me, and I lean forward to warm my hands, inhaling the scent of burned sugar from the marshmallows that have rolled into the embers. Lawrence is sitting across from me, looking slightly dazed as well. We study each other, as if one might have the answer to the other's confusion.

A stick snaps to my right. Lawrence and I turn our heads and inhale sharply at the same time. Jinn is kneeling just out of the firelight's glow, a look of defeat on his sweaty face. He's never looked more human, but then, he's never looked worse. He's shaking. He looks up at me. His mouth smiles a little, but his eyes don't—in fact, he looks like he wants to cry.

And then I remember. I cry out softly, unable to form in my throat the words I want to say—*I'm sorry, I didn't want to, I didn't mean it.* Jinn's eyes meet mine, and I'm terrified to blink for fear he might disappear. He rises from the ground and runs the last few steps between us, reaching for my hand and sweeping me up into his arms. I inhale his scent and close my eyes, letting my head rest against his chest. Lawrence is stammering apologies from behind us, but I can't hear much of anything beyond the soft beating of Jinn's heart, the sound of his breathing. I entwine my fingers in his shirt and tighten my arms around him.

"Viola," he whispers my name like it's something precious.

"I couldn't . . . I had to stop it, but I couldn't let Lawrence just . . . ," I say through the sharp feeling in the back of my throat.

"I know," Jinn answers.

"You're still here. You're staying. You have to stay. . . ." My voice shakes.

"Just for a moment," he answers, and then I realize he's glowing. It's an ever-brightening glow coming from within Jinn's body; his skin radiates warmth and brilliance, making the firelight look dingy by comparison. He's leaving. My eyes flood with tears I don't bother trying to control.

"Please, please don't go. I'll break again," I say through uneven breaths.

Jinn speaks in an unconvincing voice, smoothing my hair with one hand. "You'll be all right. You'll keep changing, healing. You're whole already, remember?"

"But more so with you. You can't . . . ," I say, my words broken apart by tears and gulps for air.

"It's what I am. I have to. I can't . . . I want to . . ." He stops speaking and kisses the top of my head.

"I'm so sorry," I mumble into his chest. Jinn lowers his head till his cheek is next to mine and raises one hand to tilt my chin toward him.

"Don't be sorry," he says, then runs his fingers down the side of my face. I want to speak—there are so many things to say—but none of them seems important right now. Jinn looks into my eyes. He glows brighter, and the arm he has around me loses a little strength. I shake my head in protest, and Jinn sighs.

His lips touch mine, and we're kissing, although I'm not sure when the kiss began. He tastes somehow of fresh air and sugar and starlight, and his lips are soft and gentle on mine. One hand strokes the side of my cheek in a way that makes me melt against him. It isn't until I open my eyes that I realize he's gone. The kiss, as seamlessly as it began, is over.

I tremble and feel cold, lifeless. Alone.

Footsteps crunch in the leaves behind me, and suddenly Lawrence's arms wrap around me. He wipes tears from my face with the back of his hand, ignoring the teardrops streaming down his own face.

"It'll be okay, Vi. You'll be okay. I just . . ." Lawrence sighs and looks back at the campfire. "I can't believe he's gone."

I frown at Lawrence. "Can't believe who is gone?"

RETURNING TO CALIBAN usually isn't as bad as being pulled *from* Caliban to the human world. When other masters made their final wishes, I welcomed the warm feeling of the Caliban sun washing over me—the way their world faded out and my own faded in. The way that, upon reaching Caliban, the sensation of aging comes to a grinding halt with the first deep breath of fresh, clean air.

But I struggle to hold on to Viola even after I feel myself slipping away. I can feel the Caliban sun on my skin, but I fight to linger in the chilly backyard. One moment longer, just one more, I think as I inhale the coconut scent of her hair. But then it's gone—she's gone, they're gone, everything is gone, and I'm on my own, staring at the violet-gold Caliban sunset.

How do you go back to a beautiful life you no longer want?

I hate to complain about it. After all, despite everything, I still love my job. I still love Caliban, even. My apartment, the sunsets, the trees, birds, the other golden-skinned jinn—it's nice to finally be visible to everyone in a room again. But there are no stars, no rain, no mall carnivals or Flamingo Dream bedrooms. And there's the raw feeling where a piece of me has been torn away, like a piece of plastic snapped off a toy, leaving behind a sharp edge.

I remember what Viola said about being whole to begin with. I was whole before I met her. I'm whole now.

Yeah, right.

Is this how she felt when she lost Lawrence? Because then it makes sense why she didn't know what to wish for to feel whole again. What is there to fix? What could possibly make me feel right?

When not delivering flowers, I spend most of my time in

my apartment, ignoring the unmade bed and the nearly bare walls. It's not unusual, for a Caliban apartment—jinn spend more time outside our homes than in them, since to us, experience is more important than nostalgia. And who is there to be nostalgic with? Rarely does anyone stick around long enough. Just the way jinn are supposed to like it.

I've now realized something: Jinn are boring.

Late in the evening, a few weeks after returning, I throw open my balcony doors and lean on the railing to watch the sunset.

There's the rushing sensation of a fellow jinn appearing behind me, just inside my apartment. I don't move; my eyes are locked on the low sun ahead. I don't want to speak to him. When the silence continues, the ifrit finally speaks to me.

"You should come out tonight."

"No."

"It'll be good for you." The ifrit steps forward and leans on the railing next to me. The city below glows with nightlife. The lights of dance clubs, the scent of restaurants preparing dinners, the sound of jinn laughing, meeting up with one another in the streets.

"I don't want to. Sorry," I respond as I turn around to lean my back against the railing.

The ifrit sighs. "I thought you'd be through with all this by now. Let it go. She's forgotten you already. Go out, find a jinn to take her place—one of your own kind. Move on."

I shake my head—how can he know so little? "I can't move on, don't you get it? Nothing moves here. I can't move here. There aren't any pieces to add to me, to cover up the place where Viola broke away. Everything about me is frozen, including the feeling of losing her."

"It'll go away," the ifrit protests.

"I don't *want* it to go away," I say through gritted teeth. No matter how badly it hurts. If it goes away, it'll be like it never happened.

The ifrit looks like he's grasping for any sense of sanity in me. "You'll probably be earthbound again before too long, so maybe then you can become . . . 'unfrozen.' You'll get past it all, and then you'll come back here to your normal—"

"I never want to be earthbound again."

"But—"

"I can never go back without wanting to see her," I say, turning to the ifrit. "So I'll go to her, at some point—if not the next time I'm earthbound, then the time after that—it'll happen, eventually. I'll watch her change, grow older without me, without even the slightest memory of me. Then I'll come back here, be frozen in time again, and return to see that she's twenty, thirty, forty. I never want to go back. It can never be like it was. I can never be like I was."

The ifrit shakes his head, looking at me like he's trying to read something in my eyes. He sighs and looks out over the city. The sun is so low in the sky that it's merely a brilliant red line on the horizon.

"You have a hearing tomorrow with the Ancient Jinn," the ifrit says in a defeated voice. "You broke all three protocols too often for them to ignore. I'll see you there." As the ifrit who pressed for my return, he's obligated to be at my hearing. I nod carelessly, and the ifrit vanishes. I don't care about the Ancients, don't care what they do to me—I knew it was coming.

I trudge inside, leaving the balcony doors open so the sounds and scents of the night can fill my room. I wrap myself in a navy-blue blanket and fall into bed, alone.

I STARE AT the canvas. Something is missing, and if I wait long enough, I'll figure out what it is.

That's it.

I grin and splash blue paint across the canvas like I'm trying to rip it apart with the bristles of my brush.

"You're still here?" Ophelia asks, smiling at me from the doorway.

"Has it been that long?" I turn to look at the clock and sigh when I realize it's almost seven. I've been in the art room since school ended. "I finished this one, though," I say, hoping to justify the hours that probably should have been used to finish my

Shakespeare homework.

"I like it, I think. It's kind of creepy, though," Ophelia says of my painting, tilting her head to the side and stepping through the door. The painting is bold and dark—night-black colored swirls, bright golden circles, and a royal blue gloss that looks silken now as it dries. All the colors feel important to me, like they're a part of me. Still, I'm having trouble putting them together correctly; they seem to belong to some greater picture I can't see clearly. Creativity—go figure.

"Anyway, do you need a ride tonight? Xander is picking me up," Ophelia says, tugging her honey-colored hair into a ponytail.

"I won't turn one down," I answer. Going to the coffeehouse where Lawrence works has become a Friday night ritual for me and a handful of other art students.

"I'll meet you out in front of the school then? I've got to run by my locker," Ophelia says. I gather my materials, ignoring the fact that my jeans are now speckled in blue paint. I'm on my way to put the paint in the supply closet when my eye catches a canvas shoved behind several others on an easel. It looks unpainted, but then I see a tiny streak of magenta. Curious, I let my supplies tumble into a pile on a table and step toward the easel. I pull the front canvases forward, letting them rest on my shoulder as I peer around to see what the rest of the fuchsia painting is.

I sigh.

This is why the art department is always broke. People waste supplies.

The painting is of a smiley face with spiky magenta hair. That's it. An entire canvas for a painting of a stick figure. I'm about to roll my eyes and walk away when something about the painting tugs at me—a memory, I think, but then I can't figure out what the memory is. Either way, I find myself grinning at the smiley face . . . yet at the same time, a strange, empty feeling washes over me. Like I've forgotten something important.

Weird. I shake my head and push the top canvases back, covering up the smiley face.

"Park Place. I believe that means you owe me all your red chips, sir," I tease Xander. He gives me a mock evil eye and passes me a stack of Connect Four chips. All the board games at the coffeehouse are missing pieces, so you have to sort of combine the remainders into one big game, then make up your own rules.

"Here, you can have my black chips," Ophelia offers, kissing him lightly on the cheek.

"I don't want your pity money," he replies, but there's no edge to his voice, and she intertwines her fingers with his lovingly.

"I'll take some pity money," Sarah Larson says, tapping her turquoise-polished fingernails on her tiny stack of chips. I slide her one of my chips and she grins. "Pity money is better than none at all."

"What are the Candyland cards for?" Lawrence asks as he sets another tray of lattes down on the table. The coffeehouse is empty except for us, and I see the other barista gathering her purse to leave.

"Those are for when you land on a Truth or Dare space," Ophelia says casually, pointing to the Chance spots on the board. Lawrence shakes his head as he drops to the floor beside my legs.

"I don't know if I even want to try and join this game," he says, eyeing the Candyland cards. "I'll just be on your team, Vi."

"Only 'cause I'm winning," I answer, nudging him with my knee.

"No kidding—you don't really expect me to join forces with Xander, do you?" Lawrence replies.

Sarah hands me the dice, which I give to Lawrence. "Go for it."

Lawrence drops the dice on the board, where they accidently scatter a few black chips placed in the center. Seven. I pick up the Scottie dog and bounce him seven spaces, to a Chance spot.

"Ah-ha, let's see," Sarah snickers, and pulls one of the Candyland cards for me. Two red blocks. "Oh, this'll be good. Double reds. Relationship-related truth question."

"How long did it take you guys to make this game up?" Lawrence says. The rest of us shrug.

"I've got one for her," Ophelia speaks up, raising an eyebrow. The other barista waves to Lawrence as she leaves, hitting the overhead lights—Xander's hair glows even brighter blue in the dim light. I cross my arms, waiting for my question.

"Okay, so I don't mean this to be awkward, but it's about Aaron," she begins. I'm surprised for a moment—the Ophelia sitting in front of me is so different from the Ollie who dated Aaron Moor, sometimes I forget they're the same person. Lawrence rolls a few of the Connect Four chips between his fingers—he isn't a big fan of rehashing my Aaron Moor days, for whatever reason.

"Not awkward at all," I reply. "But I can't know much scandal about him that you don't—you guys dated way longer than he and I did. It wasn't even a messy breakup."

"Oh, it's not about him. I was just wondering—who was the other guy?"

Lawrence chokes on his coffee. I shake my head. "There was no other guy. It just wasn't working out."

"Really? Well, that's boring," Ophelia says, grinning. "Sorry—he said something to me about it, right after you broke up . . . what was that, two, three weeks ago? Said that on the phone you told him you were in love with someone else."

"Ha," I answer. "I definitely don't remember saying that. I haven't really been in love with anyone, honestly, since handsome Laurie here." I playfully elbow Lawrence as I say that last bit.

Instead of teasing me back, like I expected, Lawrence firmly sets his coffee down on the table and jumps up. He hurriedly ducks behind the counter and grabs a broom, all but attacking the floor as he becomes very suddenly invested in sweeping. The other four of us make uncertain eye contact.

"You okay, Lawrence?" Sarah asks.

"Yeah. I just need to finish closing up," he says gruffly. The other three are fooled, but I know Lawrence better. I signal to them to give me a moment, and follow Lawrence as he disappears behind the forest-green EMPLOYEES ONLY curtain.

"Lawrence?" I say in a low voice as the heavy scent of coffee beans fills my nostrils. Lawrence turns to me, and his eyes look watery even in the room's scant lighting. He suddenly slams his hand down on one of the shelves, sending a few bottles of creamer spinning off the edge. I cringe, and he drops to the ground to pick them up.

"What's going on?" I ask as gently as I can. He stretches for one of the creamers that rolled under the wire shelves. "Lawrence, please."

"I just . . . ," he says toward the cement floor. He shakes his head. "It won't make any sense. God, sometimes I wish I could forget, too. . . ."

"Come on, at least *try* to tell me what's up," I say, lowering myself to the ground beside him. I take a creamer from his hand and wrap my fingers around his. Lawrence sighs and sits up. He squeezes my fingers lightly and pulls his hand away.

"It's . . ." He brushes a few coffee grounds off his jeans, his eyebrows furrowing like they do when he's choosing his words carefully. "It's just that it makes me . . . sad . . . to hear you say you haven't loved *anyone* since me."

"That's it?" I say, wondering if the shock registers in my voice. "That's what you're so upset about?"

Lawrence shakes his head. "I told you it wouldn't make sense. . . ."

He's got a point. I mean, I'm glad he isn't thrilled that I'm single, but punching shelves seems extreme.

"I'm sorry," he says, shaking his head like he's casting the emotion away. "You know, it's nothing. You've just done . . . you're such a good friend to me that I guess I wish you still had someone, that's all." He gathers the bottles and sets them back on the shelf in a row.

"I don't still *want* Aaron, though. And besides, I've got you and Ophelia and a handful of Connect Four chips." I grin. "I'm fine."

"Right. Sorry, Vi. Minor freakout."

"Okay, then we can go back to playing Super Monopoly Dare without you smashing things?" I say, folding my arms.

"Back to playing *what*? We really need new games," Lawrence says, rolling his eyes. There's still some hint of sorrow there; it sort of reminds me of the way I used to feel, back when I was so destroyed over breaking up with him. He steps around me and hurries back toward the board game. Still confused, I return to my circle of friends just in time to play my turn.

THIRTY
Jinn

HEARINGS AND OTHER official Caliban business are held in a beautiful building called the Centerhouse. It has bright white pillars, a silver domed top, shining windows, and elaborate murals on every wall. I shove my hands deep into my pockets and try to avoid eye contact with the dozens of jinn milling around. I've been here before, when I went through ifrit training, but never for something as unpleasant as a hearing. Especially when I know I don't have a chance of coming out unscathed.

The hearing room is large, mostly to make space for the giant table that stretches horizontally in front of me. Sitting behind it, paying little attention to me, are the Ancient Jinn. They appear to be of varying ages: one so old that his skin looks like tattered leather and his hair is shockingly white, another who looks only a decade or so older than me. Regardless, they are all centuries old, even though they may not look it; it all depends on how often they've been earthbound.

I walk to a much smaller table in the center of the room, where the ifrit is standing. We exchange glances as I come to a stop beside him. One of the Ancient Jinn—the one with the leathery skin—turns his cloudy eyes to me. I bow toward him to signal that I'm ready to begin. As ready as I'll ever be, anyway.

"Let's start, shall we?" the leathery Ancient says, his voice little more than a whisper. He is the oldest of them all, and he sits at the center of the table. He tilts his chin up to see me from beneath caterpillarlike white eyebrows.

"You have broken"—the leathery Ancient glances down at a list, and despite his thick eyebrows, I can see his eyes widen at the list's length—"*all three protocols*. Numerous times." The Ancient begins to count the offenses, tapping a pencil along the list. He flips to the next page, sighs loudly, and looks back up with an expression of disbelief. "What do you have to say for yourself?"

"Nothing," I respond, holding my hands out at my sides. "Nothing. Well, except that she commanded me to call her by name, so that shouldn't count. And she commanded me to be visible once, so . . . that, too."

The leathery Ancient looks pleased. "Ah, good. Then that brings it down to . . ." He looks at the list again, and the pleased expression disintegrates. The Ancient sighs and puts his hand to his head.

"Why break the others then? The ones that weren't a direct order?" the youngest-looking of the Ancients asks, his voice bold compared to the leathery Ancient's faded whisper.

I take a deep breath. "By choice. I broke them by choice."

A female Ancient folds her arms. "It is not our way to be a part of their world, as you tried to be. The three protocols are in place to protect not only you, but the rest of us as well. You've risked our entire livelihood. Do you want to be responsible for knowledge of our kind getting out into the human world? To see fellow jinn whisked away daily by greedy mortals?"

"No," I say softly.

"He should be bound," one of the Ancients says, giving me a cold stare. "He must repay our kind for his actions." Another Ancient agrees, then another.

Bound. Alone, imprisoned in some mortal object. I don't want to be alone. I start to feel dizzy as the other Ancients chime in.

"He's never broken protocol before, though," a younger Ancient says.

"But so many were broken this time," another responds.

"Though the number is reduced greatly when we consider the fact that his master has forgotten him."

"Still, he should be bound so that he might understand the severity of his actions."

"He's young, though. A single mistake isn't worthy of stripping him of years of his life. Before the protocols were enforced so well, we all broke them just as often."

"I certainly never broke that many."

"It's just that being bound is rather severe for a first-time offender."

The leathery Ancient interrupts the chatter. "But are there any other suggestions for how he might repay his debt to our kind?" No one speaks. One of the female Ancients gives me an especially disgusted glare.

"I have one," a voice says, falling like warm water on my frozen body. It's the ifrit. The ifrit doesn't look at me, his face firm and still.

"And it is?" the leathery Ancient asks.

The ifrit straightens his tunic. "Despite the fact that he made poor choices while earthbound, he has proven to have a heightened awareness of the human mind and condition. He once applied to be an ifrit, though he left the program. Despite this, I feel that becoming an ifrit would be a wise use of his abilities. More so than being bound on Earth."

No. I don't want to go back. I don't want to see Viola having forgotten me. And I won't be able to stay away from Viola—I know I won't. It's as bad as being bound. Worse. It'll be horrible being alone, but at least I won't have to see her without me.

The leathery Ancient frowns for a moment and runs a hand over his giant eyebrows. The other Ancients shuffle through paperwork, some nodding, others frowning. The ifrit continues to avoid my eyes.

"You believe him capable of pressing effectively? It states here that in training he wouldn't perform a fairly simple press . . . a car crash or the like . . ."

"I believe he'll have different preferences for the way he presses. As all ifrit do," the ifrit says.

"And he would have to leave his job as a flower boy—"

No. Don't make me do this.

"—to join the ifrit, naturally."

The Ancients lean across the table, mumbling to one another just out of my earshot.

"All right then," the leathery one says as the other Ancients lean back in their chairs. "It's your decision how your debt will be repaid. You can be bound in an Earth object for a period of six months or be in the service of the ifrit program for eighteen months. You will have to leave your current job, repeat the ifrit training, and prove yourself to be effective at pressing."

Six months. It's just six months. And I can return and still deliver flowers. How could I press a mortal, especially now? And how can I go back to Earth without finding her . . . without it killing me every time I see her moving, living, changing without me? It's not fair.

"Choose the job," the ifrit says to me in a nearly inaudible whisper.

"I don't want it," I reply hoarsely.

"He said he'll take the position with the ifrit, sir," the ifrit answers for me. My mouth opens to argue, but the Ancient begins speaking too soon.

"Stop by the lobby to fill out the necessary paperwork," the leathery Ancient instructs me. He snaps his fingers, and a stack of papers appears on the table in front of me. "And I hope I don't see you at a hearing again." Then the Ancient Jinn, one by one, rise and leave through a door behind the table before I can recover enough from shock to string together coherent protests. The ifrit turns on his heel and strides toward the door while my frustration paralyzes me.

How could this happen? I should never have told him

about not wanting to return. This is his personal revenge on me. My hands tremble as my anger breaks through my body's unwillingness to move, and I turn to the ifrit.

"Hey!" I shout just as the ifrit reaches the hearing room door. The ifrit turns. I grab the paperwork and run toward him, my face red and my mind reeling.

"What?" the ifrit asks.

"I trusted you! I told you those things in confidence, and you used them against me. You know I didn't want to return, and now . . . a year and a half! How could you?" I snap at him, shaking the papers in front of me.

The ifrit is silent for a moment as he studies my face. "We both know you always would have made a great ifrit. You just never liked to hurt them. They *matter* to you—they always have. I've never cared how I accomplished the press." The ifrit shakes his head, a look of wonder on his face. "I can read mortals. I can read you. You will never be happy in Caliban again, not really."

"What are you talking about?" I answer bitterly. I already know this. Believe me, I know this.

"Despite it all, you're still one of us. And as one of us, I want you to be happy, my friend. I thought you would be, once you got back home, but it isn't so. Jinn aren't supposed to feel broken, as mortals do, yet here you are, seemingly broken with no way to heal. I see it in your eyes the same way I see what's necessary to press a mortal to wish. So if the need to feel whole again is that dependent upon the girl, here you go. Full access to her, unmonitored protocol, so long as you don't forget your obligations to your kind."

I press my lips together in fury and pain. *"She's forgotten me.* It's over. I don't want to see her again, and now I'll have to. I won't be able to help it. I'll have to sit back and just watch her . . . live. Without me."

The ifrit shrugs. "Then I overestimated your feelings for her."

My jaw drops. "How *dare* you? Because I don't want to see that she's forgotten me?"

"No. Because nothing is really ever gone or forgotten. If she's a piece of you, and you of her, then memory is merely an obstacle—our power covers the memory, it doesn't erase it.

And I should think, at least based on what I saw in your eyes last night, that it's an obstacle worth going up against. Unless, of course, I overestimated your feelings for her."

I fall silent and look down, then back at the ifrit. The ifrit sighs. "I became an ifrit to save the lives of my fellow jinn. What kind of life saver would I be if I let you sit here and wither away in paradise?"

Just an obstacle. Just an obstacle.

I meet the ifrit's eyes. "What happened to all your talk about birds and fish having nowhere to live?"

The ifrit shrugs. "I suggest you start holding your breath, my friend," he says, then pushes through the hearing room doors. "I still think you're insane, for the record!" he calls out just before the doors swing shut. The breeze causes my paperwork to fly from my hands, scattering like leaves across the marble floor. I gather the papers slowly, with a strange, buzzing feeling in my heart.

THIRTY-ONE

IT'S MIDNIGHT, AND the coffeehouse closed almost an hour ago. Everyone headed home—a few to others' houses, still fewer to parties. Lawrence and I sit in his greenhouse, each of us lying on a plaid couch and watching the television via the reflection on the glass ceiling.

"I'm going to get a drink. Do you want anything?" I ask, standing and stretching my arms above my head. Lawrence, still smelling strongly of coffee and vanilla, shakes his head.

My hand meanders through the refrigerator until I come across a can of soda. I'm about to open it when I hear Lawrence's voice, muffled by distance and the sound of the

289

television. I sigh. Lawrence's mother has been clinging to the belief that Lawrence will grow out of "the gay thing" and get back together with me. Nearly every time I come over, she corners Lawrence and asks him about our "future." I'll have to go save him from her. Again.

I pause in the hallway that leads to the greenhouse, waiting for a lull in their conversation so my interruption will be smoother.

"How do you know she won't remember when she sees you?" Lawrence says in a loud whisper.

I strain to hear the response, but can't make out another speaker.

"You've been back on Earth almost a week now! You'll never know if you don't take a risk and show yourself. I hate you in that uniform, by the way—"

No one responds.

"All I'm saying is—"

"Who are you talking to?" I ask, once I've decided that there's no way Lawrence's mother is there—she's way too loud to go undetected twice. I lean against the greenhouse doorframe, eyebrows raised. Lawrence sits up quickly and looks like an animal in a car's headlights.

"Myself," he says. "Lines from a play the theater department is doing later this year."

"What play?" I ask.

"Never mind," Lawrence answers and sighs.

"What? I'm just asking." Wow. Calm down already.

"No, no, I'm not stressed at you. Just . . . I don't know. But never mind."

"Um . . . okay," I say. I realize I left my drink in the kitchen, and cast Lawrence a wary look as I turn back for it. I think he needs to lay off the espresso after closing.

"Viola."

I stop. The voice that called my name isn't Lawrence's. I whirl around.

A boy with golden skin stands beside the couch Lawrence is sitting on. He has curly black hair that's so dark it reminds me of the night sky, and he's wearing a dark blue tunic with a swirly *I* embroidered over the left chest. Clutched in one hand is a bouquet of roses; each rose is a different color—red, dark pink, peach, coral, yellow, lavender, and several in colors I didn't even know roses came in. Lawrence gives the boy a small smile before standing up beside him.

When did he come in?

The boy sets the roses on the end table. He's been holding them so tightly that all the lower leaves are crushed.

"Lawrence? Are you going to introduce me?" I ask. The way the boy stares at me, with dark, unwavering eyes, is a little unsettling. Strangers shouldn't stare this way. The boy takes a step toward me. I take one backward. He kind of freaks me out, but in a way that's more like butterflies than fear.

"You don't know him?" Lawrence asks cautiously. "Look again."

What is he getting at? I study the boy a moment longer. There's something gentle in his eyes, something that might make me smile if I weren't so confused about the whole thing. One thing I am sure of, though: I don't know him.

"Have you lost your mind?" I ask Lawrence, forcing my gaze away from the stranger.

"Look, I know I'm being weird, but just listen, all right?"

Lawrence replies. "Think. Think hard, Vi. About painting, and dating Aaron, and the mall carnival and . . . the marsh-mallow game we play. Are you sure you don't already know this guy?"

Fine. I try to focus on Lawrence's words. Painting, Aaron, carnivals, that marshmallow game. None of them has anything to do with the boy, who is now staring so hard that I fold my arms over my chest protectively.

"No," I say when I'm totally sure the boy's face doesn't exist in my memory.

"You're sure."

"Yes."

"It's fine," the boy tells me, cutting Lawrence off. Lawrence shakes his head and sighs. The boy looks at me and motions to the roses on the end table. "These are for you. I'll just . . . leave them here," he says, and touches them gingerly. He leaves his hand on them for a moment, his fingertips resting on a blue rose. There's a firm look on his face, like he's forcing himself to remain emotionless. The boy steps back and turns to leave the greenhouse by way of the door farthest from me.

"Wait, tell me who you are!" I call out after him. What's with all the secrecy? "I don't know what's so hard about this. I wish you'd give me a straight answer!" I throw my hands in the air and turn to go back to the kitchen with a sigh. Boys.

I hear the boy inhale; then he gives a halfhearted laugh as I head down the hallway.

"As you wish," he murmurs.

I turn around.

I know that. I know something about that.

I return to the greenhouse door. The boy is still standing on the opposite side of the room. My eyes dart to Lawrence, who is staring at me with a hopeful glint in his eyes.

"I know *that*," I say. "I know that, but not you. But it's familiar." I step into the greenhouse, and the scent of honey and spices floats around me. "I know all of this," I murmur. Something strange is happening; it's like Lawrence and the stranger have dredged up memories that are hidden, veiled, like the memory of a dream. The harder I try to remember, the more the memory escapes me.

"I know . . . " My voice is shaking a little in confusion.

Lawrence's eyes flit between me and the boy. "I know ... *Caliban*. Something named *Caliban*." Caliban? What's a Caliban? Why can't I remember ... ?

"Yes," the boy says breathily and takes several steps closer.

"And . . ." Something else. There's more—what is it? "And . . . the carnival. And me and Lawrence, our campfire a few weeks ago. I want to say you were there . . ."

"Yes." He takes another step. I stay put.

"And . . ." I hesitate.

"There's more," the boy says.

"That's it. That's all I remember," I reply, shaking my head. I look down at the bouquet of roses, still sitting on the end table. When I raise my eyes to look at the boy again, he's gazing at me with incredible intensity. His eyes are strange, almost like an animal's eyes—perhaps a deer's or a wolf's. He extends a hand toward me, palm open.

"That's all I remember," I repeat, but my voice is now a whisper. There's more, I know there's more. I just can't see it. I look at the boy's hand and realize that, without intending to, I'm lifting my own hand. The boy watches my fingers hungrily as they near his.

I don't know him.

My hand makes contact with his. He wraps his fingers around mine and takes a step closer. Why am I doing this? I don't know him. He looks down into my eyes like he's reading something off the back of my irises. He takes my other free hand into his own.

I shake my head. I don't know him. But his eyes are deep, his skin soft. . . .

"Viola," he says, in a voice so soft, I almost don't catch it.

I inhale sharply.

"Jinn."

The word leaves my mouth as a hopeful whisper. *Jinn.* I know this, I know all of this. I *remember.* Feelings and thoughts and memories slam into my mind, so overwhelming and brilliant that I can scarcely breathe.

I gasp for air. "Jinn," I repeat, though this time the words are pleading.

Jinn's concerned expression dissolves, and he wraps his arms around me. I bury my face into the blue silk of his ifrit uniform.

Lawrence gives a content sigh as Jinn runs a hand over my hair, and I laugh because if I don't, I'll sob.

It's several moments before I can even speak. "I forgot you," I say between shaky breaths.

"No, you didn't. The memory was just covered up. No magic can truly erase memories; it just . . . disguises them. Unless something is strong enough to reveal the truth."

I nod, but can only get one sentence to emerge from my lips: "You came back." I look into his eyes, very aware of how much like a little girl I sound. I don't care.

Jinn smiles and shakes his head, then touches my cheek tenderly. He looks into my eyes for a moment, then glances at the end table. "I was going to get you light pink roses. Admiration, friendship, romance."

"I always wanted someone to bring me flowers," I say. Though of course, he already knew that. "Why roses in every color then?"

Jinn blushes so deeply that it's visible despite his dark skin. He looks at the ceiling. "Because you . . . " He looks back into my eyes. "Because you're more to me than a single color of rose can express. You're my missing piece, Viola. I love you."

My heart swells. I inhale and pull Jinn so close that I can feel his breath on my face.

"I thought jinn didn't fall in love?" I murmur, unable to contain a smile.

He laughs lightly, eyes glittering. "So did I."

And then we kiss, holding each other, while above the greenhouse roof the stars gleam in the night.

Acknowledgments

THE ACT OF writing might be a solitary process, but the act of becoming a writer most certainly is not. A handful of people is responsible for aiding me on the journey from novice storyteller to published author, people whose guidance I would be lost without. So, I'd like to thank:

My parents, for their continued support, love, and enthusiasm, and for always encouraging me to hold fast to my dreams. Also, for doling out books like candy and allowing me plenty of late-night writing sessions. You made me strong enough to handle the journey.

My sister, Katie, for her support, laughter, and a lifetime of good memories.

My grandparents, for believing I can do anything—and convincing me of the same.

"The Box" group for making my high school experience beautiful and never doubting my ambition.

My students, both past and present, who are the greatest teachers I could ever ask for.

Jaclyn Dolamore for her wise words and support for *As You Wish* from its very first incarnation.

The 2009 Debutantes and everyone at the Blue Boards for providing shoulders to lean on and a pat on the back when I needed it most.

My agent, Jenoyne Adams, and my editor, Kristin Daly— co-conspirators in making my childhood dreams come true.

Michael O. Riley and Susan Atefat-Peckham, for giving me faith in the young-adult genre and in myself.

John Hersman, Jason Mallory, and Elizabeth Hartman, for their long-term acceptance of my craziness and their contin- ued support from one manuscript to the next.